WILD CHANCE

Wilder Irish, book 13

MARI CARR

This book (and series) is dedicated to my family—the real life Collins clan.

WILD CHANCE

Can he make this moment last a lifetime?

It's been three years since Padraig Collins lost his wife and since then, he's been sleepwalking his way through each day, focusing only on work and family, while hanging out with his best friend, Emmy.

The sum equivalent of Emmy's experience with relationships is contained within the pages of the romance novels she writes while sitting at the end of the bar at Pat's Pub. That is if she doesn't count the secret crush she's been harboring for Padraig since the first day she laid eyes on him.

When Padraig realizes he's in love with Emmy, they fall into each other's arms. However, adversity strikes and Padraig—terrified of loving and losing again—foolishly pushes Emmy away. It will take the combined romantic efforts of the entire Collins' family to help him win the heart of his best friend...and his second chance at happily ever after.

Patrick Collins took a long swig of cold Guinness and leaned back in his chair, soaking up his surroundings. His grandson, Padraig, sat across from him, grinning widely, if somewhat wearily. They'd walked the streets of Killarney for most of the morning and early afternoon until Patrick cried uncle, suggesting they break for lunch and a pint when he'd spotted what used to be Scully's Pub back in the day.

Patrick had met his wife, Sunday, at Scully's, where he'd served as the bartender. Sunday had been hired to sing and play guitar on the weekends, and it hadn't taken Patrick more than one glance of the beauty to fall madly in love.

The pub had changed hands a few times since the good old days—as Scully had passed away decades earlier—and while it had been updated a bit, it still had the same atmosphere of an old-school Irish pub.

"So you really met Grandma Sunday here?" Padraig asked.

"I did indeed. She stood right over there on that stage in the corner, picked up her guitar, and sang with the sweetest voice I'd ever heard. Took one look at her and fell head over heels."

"This is seriously cool. I can't believe I'm really in the exact same spot where you met Grandma Sunday. I gotta get a picture of this to text back to everyone else."

Padraig had always been one of Patrick's biggest fans when it came to his stories about days gone by, and his grandson had admitted last night that being able to see the actual places from all the old tales was his favorite part about their trip to Ireland.

Patrick cheesed for the camera as Padraig held up his phone, taking a selfie as the two of them pointed to the stage behind them, then his grandson texted it with the words, *Sunday's stage. First place Pop Pop ever saw her.*

Patrick anticipated that Padraig's phone would begin pinging as everyone commented about the photo. Padraig had started a family group text just before they boarded the plane to fly to Ireland for their big trip. Since then, he'd taken countless pictures to text home, after which various family members would reply. The comments made Patrick feel as if they were all there with him, and it had warmed his heart that not only was he able to share this experience with his family, but that they were all so excited to see it, so interested in his past, so curious about their roots. He was indeed blessed when it came to his children and grandchildren.

"You know, Scully's reminds me a lot of Pat's Pub," Padraig added.

The second the words crossed his grandson's lips, Patrick saw the familiar shadow fall over Padraig's face that appeared whenever the pub was mentioned.

Patrick struggled to talk about Pat's Pub as well, but he worked hard to hide that from his family. Thinking of his own beloved pub back in Baltimore, gutted by a fire a few weeks before the holidays, caused him more pain than he cared to admit. He'd been present to watch a lifetime of memories and treasures reduced to ash. The image was one he would never be able to erase, and for the first—and perhaps only—time in his life, he'd been glad Sunday hadn't been there. It would have devastated his dear wife.

Fortunately, no one had been hurt in the fire. Oliver, his grandson, as well as his partners, Gavin and Erin, who'd all been asleep in the apartment upstairs when the faulty electrical wiring sparked into flames, had managed to get out of the building via the fire escape.

The fire was actually the reason he was here now in Ireland with his son, Tris, and grandsons, Padraig and Colm. The entire family had gone together on a Christmas gift, paying for this amazing trip, no doubt to distract Patrick from the upsetting memory and to keep him busy while his other sons, Sean and Killian, worked overtime to rebuild the pub.

He hadn't returned to Ireland since he and Sunday married and moved to Baltimore over sixty years earlier, and his family had decided now was the perfect time. It was the greatest gift he'd ever received.

"Wonder what's keeping Dad and Colm," Padraig mused aloud, obviously seeking a way to change the subject.

Patrick shrugged. "Who knows with those two? At this rate, Colm is going to have to buy another suitcase to get all his trinkets, knickknacks, and treats home."

Padraig chuckled. "Yeah, well, he showed up late to the party, so he's trying to make up for lost time."

Colm, Padraig's twin brother, had joined them for the last two weeks of their six-week adventure. Unlike Padraig and Tris, who were out of work until the pub reopened, Colm had a thriving law practice he couldn't leave for such an extended period of time.

Or at least, that was the excuse he gave. In truth, Colm was a newlywed with four-month-old twins—one boy, one girl —and Patrick was shocked he'd agreed to leave them for two hours, let alone two weeks. His previously confirmed-bachelor grandson was now the most doting father and husband on the planet.

"He's determined that every single person in the family get a keepsake from Ireland. Pretty sure he's lost his mind," Padraig added. "Our family is ginormous."

While Padraig was sharing the trip through photographs and texts, Colm was finding another way to ensure everyone got to enjoy a piece of Ireland. Colm was already planning a party upon their return where he could give out presents like a Gaelic Santa Claus. "It's a nice gesture on his part and I'm sure everyone will appreciate the small gifts."

The bartender walked over to their table. "Another pint of Guinness?"

They both nodded and as the man walked away to get their drinks, Patrick took a moment to gather his thoughts before bringing up what was bound to be a difficult subject. Glancing at his grandson, he decided there was no time like the present.

"I'm glad for the opportunity to spend a few moments alone with you, lad," Patrick said. He'd been trying to steal some time with Padraig throughout the entire trip, but it had been a whirlwind of activity ever since they'd stepped off the plane in Dublin. And now...their grand journey was winding down.

"Oh?" Padraig asked, smiling his thanks as the bartender delivered their new pints and took the empty glasses away.

"I was wondering if I'd ever told you what the name Collins stands for."

Padraig's eyes widened. "Seriously, Pop Pop? I'm thirty-four years old and you're just now getting around to telling me our last name means something? You must be slipping in your old age."

Patrick laughed. "I am but a young man," he teased, beating his hand on his chest in an attempt to display his strength.

Padraig nodded his head once. "I stand corrected. For you, the nineties are at most middle age. So tell me, what does Collins mean?"

"Oh, I think you'll like this. It means young warrior."

Padraig was clearly impressed. "Seems appropriate for our family."

"That it does," Patrick agreed. "That it does."

He took another sip of his Guinness and studied Padraig's face, hoping what he said next would be received well.

Padraig had lost his beloved wife, Mia, to a brain tumor three years earlier and since then, he'd closed in on himself, simply going through the motions of daily life without truly living.

He'd wanted to talk to Padraig about his future, about the need to move on, for the past few months, but between the fire, the holidays, and now this trip, the opportunity kept slipping away from him. Now, well...there were things that simply couldn't remain unsaid. Life was too short.

Patrick could swear he sensed Sunday's spirit surrounding them right now. He glanced over at the makeshift stage and it seemed as if she was standing there, guitar in one hand, the other on her hip, giving Patrick *that* look that told him to pull his thumb out. Their grandson needed some tough love.

"It's time to put down the shield, Paddy, and pick your weapon back up."

"What?" Padraig asked.

"You've been nursing your wounds too long, lad."

"Pop Pop—" Padraig started, but Patrick put his hand up and shook his head.

"You've spent the past three years holding a shield in front of you. That's not the way of a young warrior. Because it isn't protecting you in battle. That's not the way you're using it. You're hiding behind it. Pure and simple. It's time to drop it, pick up your sword, and love again."

"Are you seriously comparing love to war?" Padraig joked, though Patrick could tell his words were striking a chord.

"Yes. I am. Because it is a war you're waging. Problem is… it's the wrong one. I understand that you're wrestling with grief and struggling with depression. That's normal. But you're also drowning in a sea of guilt."

"Guilt?"

Patrick nodded, unsurprised that was the description that confused Padraig. It proved just how hard his grandson was still fighting against something that was clear as day to anyone else with eyes. "Mia never asked you to grieve for her forever. In fact, I recall that lovely woman asking you for the opposite."

"It's not that easy, Pop Pop."

"I never said it was. But…it's also not impossible, something I think you already know. And that's what's causing the guilt you're feeling."

Padraig took a deep breath but remained silent.

Patrick waited him out, forcing his grandson to face something he'd been fighting like the devil to ignore, to deny.

No…not something.

Someone.

While Padraig might still be closing his eyes to the truth, Patrick could see it crystal clear.

Padraig took another sip of his pint as he glanced out the window. "Okay," he said at last. "Okay. You're right. I need to move on. And I will. Soon. I just...I'm not sure..."

"Paddy. You can do this."

Padraig didn't look wholly convinced, something Patrick could understand and appreciate. The pain of losing Sunday had gutted Patrick, but he'd been older. He'd had many, many wonderful years with his wife, and they'd created a beautiful family together. He'd had his children—and then grandchildren—to sustain him, to fill his life with joy and love.

Padraig was still a young man, one with a lot of love to give to another woman and—God willing—to children of his own. In the years since Mia's passing, he'd thrown himself into work, pretending that the job was enough. However, since the fire, Padraig didn't even have the pub to get him through each day, so the shadows caused by his depression came more frequently, lasted longer, were darker.

"Sometimes I feel guilty," Padraig confessed. "Guilty that I'm still here, still alive, when Mia's gone. What right do I have to move on when she doesn't have that option?"

"No. You're looking at this the wrong way. You owe it to Mia to live your life to the fullest. To do otherwise is disrespectful to her memory. She didn't want you to stop when she did. You know that because she said it to you. Over and over."

"I know." Padraig ran a hand through his hair, frustration rife in his eyes. "I know she did. But it doesn't make this any easier."

"I never said it would be easy. But you can do this. I believe that with all my heart."

Padraig sighed sadly, but Patrick could tell he was thinking about what he'd said. The seed had been planted. With any luck, it would take root and his grandson would reach out for his second chance at happiness.

Because Patrick didn't doubt for a moment, it was there.

She was there.

All Padraig had to do was open his eyes and his heart and see her.

Patrick smiled and placed his hand on top of Padraig's. "Be brave, my young warrior."

❧   I   ❧

Emmy lay on her couch, staring at the blinking Christmas lights as her kitty, Luna, nestled next to her. Her other cat, Neville, was asleep at her feet, purring loudly. It was her third Christmas Eve alone, something that never got any easier. She was a people person by nature with more than her fair share of FOMO, so spending any holiday alone sucked.

She'd called her brother, Sam, earlier in the day. He was in year two of a five-year stint in prison, incarcerated for selling drugs. The five-minute phone call was predictably awkward as she attempted to find cheerful, uplifting things to say. Things that were met with Sam's usual reply—either silence or the occasional grunt that let her know the phone call hadn't been disconnected.

After that, she'd treated herself to steak and French fries, as well as an entire bottle of Chardonnay, unconventional holiday fare but her favorite dinner. She'd hoped the wine would allow her to simply pass out until Christmas Day, when—thank God—she actually had plans that included socializing with fun people.

Her best friend, Padraig, had invited her to spend the day with his family tomorrow, a gift of immeasurable value as far as she was concerned. She'd been invited the previous year, and the memory of that day never failed to bring a smile to her face. The Collins clan did the holidays right, and it saved her from reliving that first Christmas alone for a second time.

Her mother had passed away when Emmy was twenty-three, then her father had suffered a massive heart attack just before Thanksgiving three years earlier and her brother had been MIA at the time. She'd spent that entire Christmas alone, looking at old family photos and crying into her wine.

She'd vowed she was never going to let herself drift back to that dark place and had actually researched cruises, thinking she could spend the holidays drinking mai tais on some Caribbean beach, and flirting with some hot island waiter.

When Padraig invited her to Christmas with his family, she decided that was a much better offer. She was crazy about the Collins family...and Padraig. She'd always known that he wasn't looking for a relationship, wasn't interested in dating, so she'd tucked her attraction away.

However, as more time passed, their *just friends* state was beginning to chafe.

Her phone rang, rousing her from her melancholy state. "Speak of the devil," she murmured to herself when Padraig's face appeared on the screen.

"Happy Christmas Eve," she said as she answered, forcing as much cheerfulness into her voice as she could muster.

"Right back atcha," Padraig said with a chuckle, his tone more natural than hers. "Having a good night?"

"Yeah. It was great," she lied. "How was dinner at your parents' house?" she asked, hoping to deflect before he asked for details about her less-than-great night.

"The same as always. Loud—thanks to Kelli and Colm. And this year, with the addition of the twins, I'm pretty sure I have permanent hearing damage."

She laughed. "If you haven't suffered hearing loss from your family before now, I suspect you'll recover just fine."

"Still on for tomorrow?" he asked.

"Of course," she quickly replied. "I wouldn't miss it for the world."

"Good. We've got a big surprise for Pop Pop this year. Something we're hoping will take his mind off the pub."

Emmy swallowed heavily to dislodge the lump in her throat that appeared whenever she thought about the fire that had ravaged Pat's Pub just a few weeks earlier. "What is it?"

"Nope. Not telling. I know how susceptible you are to Pop Pop's charms. If he figures out something's up, you'll be the first one he questions."

Emmy grinned with amusement but didn't bother to deny it. "I'd like to defend myself against that, but who are we fooling? That man bats those chocolate-brown eyes at me and I forget my own name."

"Celebration starts at one," he reminded her, though it wasn't necessary. She'd had the date and time circled on her calendar for months.

"I was thinking," she said, the wine prompting her to speak before her too-reasonable brain could shut her up.

"Yeah?"

"Would you want to go out sometime...after the holidays?"

"We go out all the time, Em."

Emmy had two choices.

Backpedal or forge on.

The queen of backpedaling when it came to Padraig, she actually shocked herself when she said, "I mean on a date."

Chardonnay for the win.

"Oh." And then there was a pause. "Em." Another pause—this one more painful than the one before.

She started to let him off the hook. To tell him to forget it. To blame the wine. But she held her tongue. Because she was tired of pretending...of hiding...of playing things cool.

"Em. I'm sorry, but I don't think that's…I'm not ready to start dating again. I think it's better if we just stay friends."

The part of her that lacked all self-preservation held on for a split second, waiting, wishing, wanting him to add two more words to that assertion.

For now.

If he would include for now…*she would keep waiting. God, part of her feared she'd wait forever if he said those words.*

But he didn't say them.

"Okay. Yeah. I didn't meant to…I…I'm sorry, Paddy. Too much wine tonight. Went straight to my head," she said, trying to make light of her disappointment and failing pretty spectacularly. She dug deeper and managed to pull just-friends Emmy out of the rubble. "It's totally cool. Honest. We're always going to be great friends."

"Best friends," he added quietly.

"Best friends," she agreed, wishing that made her feel better. "I'll see you tomorrow, okay?"

The silence that followed told her he wanted to say more, but, like her, it appeared he didn't know how to recover from this. So he let them both off easy.

"Sure thing. See you tomorrow."

EMMY SAT IN HER CAR OUTSIDE THE RESTAURANT FOR A moment, trying to get out of her head, wishing she wasn't still hung up on that damn phone call from Christmas Eve.

Five weeks had passed, but the memory of that conversation kept coming back to her, playing itself over and over in her brain. That night, while devastating, had been a wake-up call, a turning point, because she realized just how pathetic she'd become, hoping to win the heart of a man who'd already given his to someone else.

She'd spent Christmas with the Collins family, managing

to put her and Padraig back on steady footing, joking around, keeping things casual. By tacit agreement, neither of them mentioned the phone call, instead falling right back into their normal fun-loving friendship.

But since the holidays, she'd doubled down on sorting her shit out. She had a definite vision of her future and it was way past time she found a way to get there, instead of sitting at the end of a bar, pining for her best friend.

This was going to be *her* year.

Of course, that determination hadn't really been tested because she hadn't seen Padraig since Christmas Day. He'd left for a grand tour of Ireland just a few days after. The two of them had maintained the status quo on their relationship through texts and phone calls. And now, Padraig was in the last week of his six-week trip with his grandfather, dad, and brother.

She'd put the weeks away from him to good use.

Or at least, she hoped so. Only time would tell.

She glanced up at Kelli's favorite Mexican restaurant, wishing for the thousandth time that she was meeting her friends at their usual stomping ground, Pat's Pub. It had been a long winter for Emmy since the place she'd come to consider her second home—actually, she was there so much, it was probably her first home—had been closed down following the fire.

She shook off that sadness, trying to comfort herself with the knowledge that the Collins family, who owned and operated the pub, were rebuilding it and, according to Padraig—during their last text exchange—it was slated to reopen just a couple weeks after he returned home from Ireland.

She got out of her car and crossed the street. Entering the restaurant, she glanced around, then grinned when she spotted her friends.

Sometimes she was amazed how much her life had changed in just two years. And she had the table full of women waiting for her, as well as the entire Collins family, to thank for that.

Ever since she'd walked into Pat's Pub that first time, nothing had been the same.

Thank goodness.

Her journey to the pub that initial time hadn't been intentional or thought out. Instead, it felt like karma, or perhaps the spirit of her parents, had led her there. After all, Mom and Dad had met at Pat's Pub, set up on a blind date by mutual friends.

Her reason for venturing out of her apartment two years prior had been driven by a celebration after she'd achieved a pretty major life goal. Every second of that day was etched so deeply in her memory, it could have happened yesterday.

She'd woken up to find an email from one of her super-fans, telling her she'd made *The New York Times* best seller list. She'd begun writing romance novels when she was a teenager, and she'd sold her first book when she was just twenty. In the seven years since that first sale, she'd managed to make a name for herself, as well as more than enough money to live on after both her parents' passing.

Emmy had been certain the reader was mistaken about her hitting the list.

But nope.

It had been the truth. Her book was right there at number nine.

Her immediate flash of indescribable joy was instantly dashed. She'd accomplished a major life goal—maybe the biggest—and...

She hadn't had a single soul to share it with.

She'd thought of her parents, of course, wishing they were

still alive. Her mother—in her healthy years—would have flipped out, put on music, danced around the apartment, and then made Emmy a four-layer chocolate cake to celebrate. Her father would have hugged her, bought her flowers, and told her how proud he was of her.

But without them...

Loneliness hadn't been a stranger to her, but that was the first time it crushed her. The first time it felt truly unbearable.

Emmy had turned a corner *that* day as well, aware that at some point, she'd dropped the reins on her life and had failed to pick them back up. So she'd walked away from her computer, gotten dressed in real clothes—rather than her usual loungewear—and headed outside. She'd decided to treat herself to lunch, not takeout or delivery, but to a real meal in a real restaurant.

She'd walked into Pat's Pub and boom!

New life, new friends, newfound happiness.

Emmy was certain the Collins family didn't have a clue how much they'd impacted her world, changing it for the better.

"Emmy!" Kelli called out from across the restaurant, her loud voice drawing the attention of pretty much everyone in the place. "Get your ass over here. We're halfway through the first pitcher of margaritas."

Emmy grinned when the patrons' gazes slid from Kelli to her as she made her way across the restaurant. Kelli Collins had a booming voice, a boisterous laugh, and one of those personalities that drew people in like moths to a flame.

"You started without me?" she asked, gesturing to the margaritas in front of them as she hung her winter coat on a hook next to the large corner booth her friends had claimed.

"You're late," Sunnie said, just before popping a chip

covered with salsa into her mouth. "And the only reason there's still half a pitcher left is because I'm pregnant."

Emmy looked at her watch. "I'm five minutes late."

Caitlyn waved her hand as if that only proved Sunnie's point. "She's not wrong about her pregnancy slowing down our pace. You're going to have to pick up the slack."

Emmy shook her head in amusement, then sat down and thanked Kelli, who'd picked up the margarita pitcher and filled a glass for her. "I'm not a suitable stand-in for Sunnie. Only had two of these the last time and my head ached for days afterwards. They're wicked strong."

"After all this time with us, you'd think you would have built up some kind of tolerance for margaritas," Caitlyn mused, winking at her.

Kelli topped up her own glass and Yvonne's to empty the pitcher before waving to the waitress to order another.

"Where are Layla and Erin?" Emmy asked, aware they were a few girlfriends short on the monthly margarita happy hour.

"The Italian Stallions are in town today, consulting with Uncle Justin and Uncle Killian on the pub rebuild. They're ready to start putting in the furnishings and decorations," Sunnie replied, using her mother Riley's nickname for the super-sexy Moretti brothers from Philadelphia.

Moretti Brothers Restorations was an incredibly successful business known for their amazing skill at home and business renovations. They'd been featured more than a few times on various shows on HGTV. Of course, Emmy figured the fact that the business was run by four of the hottest guys on the planet probably helped get them on television as much as their mad carpentry skills.

"They're already on the decorating phase?" Emmy asked, wondering why she was so surprised to discover how quickly things were moving on the pub. The Collins family was a force of nature and the pub was the nucleus of their universe, so it stood to reason none of them would rest until it was put back to rights.

"Already," Yvonne said with a huge grin. "You should see the kitchen. It's a dream. State-of-the-art everything." Yvonne, along with her aunt Riley, served as cooks for the pub, as well as the connecting restaurant, Sunday's Side.

"Anyway, Layla and Erin and their guys are joining Layla's brothers for drinks and dinner after the meeting," Sunnie added. "Layla bitches nonstop about her overprotective brothers coming to Baltimore to check up on her too much, but damn if she doesn't stop everything to spend time with them when they hit town."

If Emmy had brothers like Layla, rather than the one she had, she'd be exactly the same way, putting everything aside to spend time with them. The Morettis were a close-knit family, very much like the Collinses.

"And where's Darcy? She never misses," Emmy said after taking a sip of her margarita.

"She's caught some sort of stomach bug," Sunnie replied. "Which means we're just going to have to double down on the 'when are you getting pregnant?' portion of happy hour next month."

Darcy, who'd married the love her life, Ryder, last summer, insisted she was in no hurry to have children because Clint, Ryder's son from his previous marriage, was more than enough for them at the moment. Puberty had hit, and apparently Clint was giving her and Ryder a run for their money when it came to moodiness.

Sometimes the size of the Collins family overwhelmed Emmy. There were countless aunts, uncles, cousins, spouses, and now, an ever-growing brood of babies. Emmy had counted nearly fifty people at Christmas before she gave up. A Collins Christmas was a far cry from her holidays growing up, which had consisted of just her, her mom, her dad, and sometimes—if he'd bothered to come home—her older brother, Sam.

"Are you missing Colm?" Emmy asked Kelli.

Kelli gave her an incredulous look. "He's only been in Ireland a week. That's not nearly enough time to miss that asshole."

Everyone laughed at the joke, though no one was fooled by it at all. Kelli and Colm had grown up together, spent nearly a lifetime as "frenemies" before succumbing to what Colm referred to as the Collins curse a year ago.

According to Colm, whenever someone in his family fell in love, it was fast, hard, and forever.

Emmy had laughed the first time Colm told her about the "curse," and she'd even gone so far as to include the concept in one of her romance novels.

Lately though, she was less amused by it, hung up on the one word in the curse that did indeed feel like...well...a curse.

Forever.

"Sleeping in his shirts?" Sunnie asked Kelli, proving exactly what Emmy had known as well.

Kelli sighed. "Every damn night. Last night, I spritzed some of his cologne on his pillow. When did I become such a hopeless case?"

"I think the phrase is hopeless romantic," Emmy said.

Kelli rolled her eyes. "I stand by what I said."

"Where are the twins?" Emmy asked.

Kelli took another sip of her margarita. "With their grandma Lane, who actually issued a threat when I left, telling me she wanted those babies to herself for at least three hours, so y'all gird your loins. I intend to take her up on that, which means this happy hour is gonna be a marathon, not a sprint."

Yvonne rubbed her forehead. "Ugh. I can already feel tomorrow's hangover coming on."

Caitlyn sighed. "It's been ages since I've seen you girls. Not since Christmas. I'll be glad when the pub reopens. I hate not knowing anything about what you all are up to."

Emmy also felt out of touch with her friends. Ever since the fire, she'd been forced back into her apartment. During her childhood, her family's apartment had been her happy place, but nowadays, it felt as if the walls were closing in on her, the apartment too small, too quiet, too boring.

Too lonely.

"I agree. So," Yvonne continued, "what has everyone been doing? Let's catch up."

Sunnie grinned. "Landon and I have been painting-and-decorating fools. The nursery is already ready for this little munchkin and he's not showing up until May."

"He?" Emmy asked. "Did I miss something?"

Yvonne and Kelli also perked up.

"If you did, we did too. It's a boy?" Kelli asked excitedly.

Sunnie grinned and nodded. "Yep. Aaron Jackson Riggs will be here before we know it. We're naming him after my dad, and he completely flipped out when we told him. I think he might have cried a little bit. We're planning to call him AJ."

They all lifted their glasses—four margaritas and one iced tea—and clinked out a toast to baby AJ, as Sunnie filled them in on the nursery's color scheme and theme. Kelli suggested several baby must-haves Sunnie needed to include on her baby shower registry. Yvonne and Caitlyn chimed in as well.

Typically, Emmy loved listening to all of their family/husband/kid stories, but today it was reinforcing the desire she'd been unable to shake the past few months. It was definitely time for her to take control of her life.

Topping up their glasses yet again—Emmy was really going to pay for this tomorrow—Kelli turned her attention to Emmy. "Okay, your turn, girlfriend. What have you been doing since the holidays?"

"Two things, actually."

"Ooooo...I love it. Lots to share. Spill," Sunnie insisted.

"First of all, I hit *The New York Times* best seller list again."

Everyone at the table cheered, and Yvonne admonished Emmy for not telling them that the second she sat down. She'd hit the list three times since her first visit to Pat's Pub, and the Collins family always made her feel like a million bucks. Every single time, Riley baked her a cake, while the others bought her drinks at the pub, toasting "her brilliance."

Kelli leaned forward, her face filled with mischief. "You do realize I've been stockpiling the *Times*, and I'm," she pinched her thumb and index fingers tightly together, "this close to figuring out your pen name."

Emmy laughed. "Which is why I never tell you I've hit it on the actual week I make the list. Let's just say I was on the list sometime in the last month...or three."

Kelli groaned and good-naturedly called her a bitch.

No one in the Collins family—with the exception of their grandfather, Patrick—knew her pen name. Originally, she'd held back telling them because her romance novels were spicy and she'd been a little embarrassed. Not of what she'd written but of how the Collins family might use that knowledge. In addition to their love of betting, they were experts when it came to teasing and practical jokes. She could just imagine Kelli and Colm standing up at the pub one night to do a dramatic reading from one of her bedroom scenes.

Lately, however, she was withholding the name simply because it was fun. They were all working overtime to try to discover it, and she didn't doubt for a moment there was some sort of betting pool running over who would figure it out first.

Sunnie fired off a text. "I told Mom to start baking your cake. Told her to go red velvet this time. I'm having a craving for red velvet. So you have to share it with me."

"That was only one thing. What's the other?" Caitlyn prompted. "Because I'm not sure you can top that news."

Emmy forced a grin, perfectly aware her next words were probably going to shock everyone at the table. "I've started online dating."

As she expected, all four of her friends erupted.

"What?" Sunnie asked. At the same time Yvonne shouted, "When?"

"Have you actually been going out on dates?" Kelli chimed in, barreling over the other women's questions.

Emmy shook her head. "Not yet. I've just been messaging with a few guys, but, well, I think I'm ready to progress to the next stage. Going to propose face-to-face meetings the next time I chat with each of them."

"Them?" Yvonne asked.

"I've been talking to three men."

"Three different guys?" Sunnie asked, Emmy pleased to hear a definite "impressed" tone.

"Yes. They all seem super nice and haven't given off a creepy vibe."

Yvonne laughed. "God. How many creeps did you have to sift through to narrow it down to those three?"

Emmy blew out a long breath. "Too many. I'd tell you about some of the dick pics random guys sent me, but I've had to work overtime—and drink a lot of wine—to erase them from my memory."

Sunnie scoffed. "I will never understand why some men think women want to see their freaking dicks. I mean, who even told these guys that wrinkly, hairy appendage is attractive?"

"I have no idea," Emmy replied sincerely. "But I swear the second I mentioned I was a romance writer, no less than five guys followed that pronouncement up with a picture of what they all assumed would serve as great inspiration for my next book. So gross. Needless to say, that's when those conversations ended."

"Damn right. So...I'm curious. When's the last time you went out on a date?" Yvonne asked.

Emmy had expected this question. Mainly because since meeting and befriending these women, Emmy hadn't been on a single date. Instead, she'd spent practically every day sitting at the end of the bar at Pat's Pub, trying—and failing—to hide the fact she'd fallen in love with their cousin, Padraig.

Dating was one of those things that fell off the radar about the same time she'd dropped the reins on her life. Her world had imploded slowly over the span of eight years, beginning with her mother being diagnosed with ALS when Emmy was seventeen, dying of the horrible disease shortly after Emmy turned twenty-three, followed by her dad's massive heart attack, and then her brother being sentenced to prison.

But the details about her mother's disease wasn't something she'd ever come out and talked to her girlfriends about. Her friends knew both her parents had passed away, but Emmy had never gone into much detail.

Padraig—whom she considered the best friend she'd ever had—knew a bit more about her family issues because they spent a lot of time together and, true to the cliché about bartenders, he was a great listener and very easy to talk to.

As such, he knew how her parents had died, the fact her brother was in jail, all the nitty-gritty details of her career writing and publishing romance novels, except for her pen name. He also knew she was crazy about her cats, loved white wine, and that she was obsessed with Hallmark Christmas movies.

Honestly, Padraig knew more about her than anyone else in the world, but there were still parts of herself—big parts—that she'd held back, hidden from even him.

Like what she was about to confess now.

"I haven't been on a date in nearly three years. And I haven't had a real boyfriend since high school," she admitted, fighting the urge to giggle when the table went unusually quiet.

"High school?" Yvonne asked.

"Yep. I was seventeen. His name was Brandon. It was love at first sight and lasted about four months," she emphasized. "Practically a lifetime in high school years."

These women were never at a loss for words, so the current silence was pretty amusing.

Sunnie, of course, recovered first. And, in typical fashion, jumped straight to the big question, ignoring the thirty-seven thousand others she could have asked first to ease them into this. "Emmy. Are you a virgin?"

"Wow. You went straight for the jugular," Emmy said, hoping the joke would ease the sudden seriousness on all their faces.

Sadly, no one laughed.

To heck with it, she thought. She'd come here today determined that she was going to open up to these women because she needed advice and encouragement. "No, Sunnie. I'm not. I've had sex."

"With Brandon?" Yvonne asked.

"Yeah. He was my first."

"But was he your last?" Kelli tossed out.

Emmy sighed. "No. He wasn't. I had a one-night stand shortly after my mom died that I totally regret. It was driven by grief and a fuck ton of tequila. And then the guy I went out with a few years ago."

"Define a few years ago," Yvonne said.

"Four years."

"And nothing since then?" Kelli asked for clarification.

"Holy shit," Sunnie cried. "I'm pretty sure the hymen grows back after three years."

Emmy rolled her eyes and laughed. "Shut up. It does not."

"Why three years?" Kelli asked Sunnie.

"I don't know. It just sounds right to me," she replied confidently.

Kelli laughed and chucked a tortilla chip at Sunnie. "You are so fucking random."

"But, Emmy, you write romance," Yvonne said, her brow furrowed, as if she was struggling to put the pieces of a puzzle together. "I thought you said they were sexy romance stories."

"They *are* sexy," Emmy replied. "Very sexy."

"How do you describe," Yvonne waved her hands around, then leaned closer, whispering, "orgasms if you haven't had one in a million years?"

"Let's just say I've done research. *A lot* of research."

Kelli burst out laughing. "Oh my God. You just totally admitted to watching a ton of porn. What's your go-to search? Bondage? Anal? Gang bang? Wait. I bet you're a hentai girl."

"*I'm* random?" Sunnie blurted.

Emmy rolled her eyes. "I'm not admitting to any of that."

"Gotcha," Kelli said smugly. "All of it. Kinky bitch. I love it."

Emmy didn't need a mirror to know she was blushing like a fiend. Regardless, she wanted to tell her friends everything because once she started going out on honest-to-God real dates again, she was going to need their guidance. She'd taken herself off the market for way too long.

"I've had orgasms, Vonnie. With all three of the guys, and since then, a ton of self-induced ones. I'm a writer—my imagination is fairly huge. You know as well as I do, you don't need a man to have an orgasm. Just a hot fantasy world, an hour or two to rewatch that honeymoon scene in *Outlander*, and some good sex toys."

Emmy enjoyed the raucous laughter her words produced. Her role within the group was usually that of the quiet friend, while the other ladies told the risqué jokes and stories that had her in stitches. It felt good to be on this side of the conversation for once—to be the one who was bold and audacious and funny.

"This might be the greatest margarita date yet," Kelli proclaimed. "Layla, Erin, and Darcy are going to be pissed they missed it."

"So to recap for those not in attendance," Sunnie said, a twinkle in her eye that said she was enjoying this all way too much. "Our sweet-as-pie friend Emmy is a born-again virgin romance writer with an arsenal of sex toys and a sketchy-as-hell internet history. Does that sum it up about right?"

"You nailed it," Kelli said.

"I'm confused," Caitlyn said. It wasn't until she spoke that Emmy realized Caitlyn hadn't added anything to their conversation.

"What are you confused about?" Emmy asked.

"Why online dating? Why not Paddy?" Caitlyn asked.

Emmy wasn't sure how to respond. She'd thought Sunnie's virginity question was going to be the most difficult one to answer, but Caitlyn had blown that out of the water.

Of course, it wasn't as if Emmy didn't have an answer. It

was the answer to that very question that led her to online dating. "We're just friends, Cait."

Sunnie didn't let that answer lie. "So were Landon and I. And Yvonne and Leo. That *just friends* thing doesn't cut it at this table."

"Maybe not, but he's not ready."

Padraig had been a grieving widower for just over a year when Emmy met him. And while she'd never met his wife, Mia, Emmy felt like she knew the woman. Because of Padraig's occasional comments about her and the stories the Collins family told. Mia had obviously been an incredible person and she had won the heart not only of Padraig but his entire family. Their fondness for her and the way they all missed her touched and broke Emmy's heart simultaneously. Mia had left a huge hole when she passed away, one that she wasn't certain Padraig would ever attempt to fill again.

Kelli tilted her head, considering the response. "I disagree. I think he *is* ready."

Emmy was certain Kelli didn't have a clue how much those words hurt. No doubt her friend was trying to give her hope where there was none.

"No, he's not," Emmy said quietly.

Kelli never gave up easily. "Yeah, but how do you know that for su—"

"He told me," Emmy cut in. "I asked him out on a date and he said he wasn't ready. Said we couldn't be more than friends."

"When did you ask him out?" Sunnie asked. "Because maybe he's changed his mind since then."

"Christmas Eve."

"Oh," Sunnie whispered.

For the second time today, Emmy managed to render the table silent. This might be a record.

Caitlyn recovered first, the lawyer in her clearly searching for a loophole. "He really said those words? Just friends?"

Emmy nodded. "Yeah, so I'm moving on. For him and for me. I don't want to lose his friendship, and I'm afraid it'll drive a wedge between us if he thinks I'm pining for him."

No one bothered to refute that statement. And while in her head, Emmy may have accepted that Padraig was never going to feel for her what he felt for Mia, her heart would take a little longer to catch up.

"So..." she said, pasting on a cheerful smile. "I think it's time for me to accept that fact and move on. Actually, I've *already* accepted that," she lied. "And I'm excited about meeting these other guys."

No one looked convinced. She was obviously a lousy liar.

But it didn't matter. She'd put the time Padraig was in Ireland to good use. Signing up for the dating app, creating a profile, and putting herself out there, while really thinking about what she wanted her future to look like.

She glanced around the table at each of them. "I want what you have," Emmy admitted. "To fall in love with a man who falls right back. Marriage. Babies. My very own happily ever after. I can't keep living vicariously through the characters in my books. It's time for something real. Not...imaginary."

She was fairly certain every woman at the table knew exactly what she meant by imaginary. She wasn't talking about her books. She was talking about Padraig.

"Then that's what we're going to get you," Sunnie said, slapping her hand on the table.

"Hear! Hear!" Kelli lifted her glass. "There's a fourth-grade teacher at my school who's single. He's pretty cute and great with kids. I'll set you up."

"Oh!" Caitlyn chimed in. "There's an awesome guy who works for Lucas who'd be perfect for you."

"I'm going to check with Landon, see if there are any hot single cops at the precinct," Sunnie added.

Emmy raised her hands. "Wait. I already have the three guys I'm talking to on the dating app."

Yvonne sighed. "Oh, babe. You're going to have to trust us. You'll kiss a lot of frogs before you find that Prince Charming. Keep all your options open. Let them set you up."

And this was why Emmy had come to her friends.

"Okay. Let's do it. Set me up with all of them."

❧   2   ❧

Padraig stood next to the bar at the pub, his eyes studying the nameplate that proclaimed this spot was reserved for Emmy. There'd been a similar nameplate on the original bar. Padraig could still recall Emmy's face when he'd unveiled it to her a year or so earlier. Her entire face had lit up with delight and she'd nearly fallen over the bar as she'd hugged him.

"What do you think?"

Padraig looked up at Tony Moretti's question, his gaze sliding around the pub once more. He'd been back home for seven days—after the whirlwind six weeks in Ireland—and he was still blown away by the fact he was standing here...in the pub.

It was as if his uncles and the Morettis has resurrected the place from the ashes, managing to put it back almost exactly as it had been before the fire. While they still had a bit more work to do, the majority of the pub was there, the walls painted, the floors sanded and stained, the booths and tables filling the space, the pennants, tin signs, framed family pictures as well as autographed ones from the Collins celebrities—Sky, Teagan, Aubrey, and Hunter—were hanging up in almost exactly the same places as before.

But best of all, the long mahogany counter was back, the brass plates marking the two spots permanently reserved for Pop Pop and Emmy, gleaming brightly.

Now, his uncles had moved on to the apartment upstairs, working to restore the two floors above them, while the Moretti brothers finished working their magic on the pub and adjoining restaurant. They were in the process of decorating Sunday's Side.

Tony, the oldest Moretti brother, had reassured them that they could recreate the pub's look, and after seeing this mahogany bar, Padraig was convinced the men possessed magical abilities.

The youngest brother, Gio Moretti, was a master carpenter and he'd somehow managed to completely recreate the counter, the new one so much like the original, Padraig had done a double take when he'd first walked in this morning and seen it.

"This place looks amazing, Tony. I can't begin..." Padraig fought to find the words. He'd spent every single day since the fire struggling to keep his head up, devastated by all his family had lost. Now...that misery was gone. "Gio did an amazing job recreating the mahogany bar. I can't believe it's not the same one."

Tony smiled. "I'll be sure to tell him you said that. He'll be relieved to know you're pleased. He knew it was the most important piece of furniture in the place, the one thing that really needed to be done right, so he's been working on it pretty much around the clock."

"He nailed it. More than nailed it."

"Tony. You have a minute? Want to see if we can shift one

of these booths a bit," Aunt Keira called out through the opening between the pub and Sunday's Side.

"Duty calls," Tony said, crossing the room and disappearing into the restaurant.

Padraig ran his hand over the counter, aware that anyone who saw him now would probably think him unhinged, grinning like a damn fool over a bar.

He, Pop Pop, Colm, and Dad had returned from Ireland the week before. He'd stopped by Finn's place to pick up his dog, Seamus, before heading to his apartment to unpack, do laundry, and fight to stay awake, so as to ward off the jet lag. Not that he'd managed. It had taken him two days to readjust to the time difference, and since then, he'd spent every moment from morning to evening here in the pub, working.

His gaze landed on Emmy's brass nameplate once more, and he reached for his phone. Before the fire, he saw Emmy nearly every damn day as she set up camp here in her spot to write romance novels. He'd missed her more than he thought he would. They'd spoken on the phone a few times since his return, but because he was working such long hours, they hadn't managed to actually get together.

She sounded somewhat breathless when she answered. "Hey, stranger. What's up?"

He grinned. "Guess where I am."

"I'm going to go out on a limb and say the same place you've been since you got back. The pub."

He chuckled. "Be more specific, please."

She paused, stumped, and then he heard her intake of breath. "Oh my God. Did Gio finish the bar? Are you standing behind it?"

"Nope. I'm standing next to your spot, complete with the brass plate that reads Reserved for Emmy Martin."

"No way. You had them put the nameplate back on it?"

"Of course I did."

"You have to take a picture and text it to me. Right now."

Emmy knew how devastated Padraig had been by the fire. Mainly because she'd shared in that pain. She loved the place almost as much as he did.

"What if we do one better? Why don't you come over and see for yourself? I'm going to be here working until the wee hours again. Bring your laptop if you want."

"Are the Morettis there?" she asked.

He knew exactly why she was asking. Ordinarily he would have laughed and teased her, but this time...his mind drifted back to what Pop Pop had said to him in Ireland. It was obvious his grandfather thought Emmy was Padraig's second chance at happiness, and the more Padraig considered that, the more he wondered if Pop Pop was right.

"They're here," he said.

"Is Tony wearing his hair down?"

Padraig glanced across the pub to where Tony was talking to Keira. The man's long brown hair was down, hanging loose. The subject of Tony Moretti's hair seemed to enthrall every female in his family, as well as Emmy. Riley and Bubbles fanned themselves behind Tony's back every time he walked past them.

"It's down," he grumbled, fighting hard to give her the feigned much-aggrieved tone that was part of this friendly song and dance between them.

"Damn. I'm so tempted. Tony and his brothers have inspired at least a few dozen romance heroes for me." She sighed dramatically, but he was too hung up on her words to tease her for her crush like he normally would.

She didn't intend to accept his invitation.

"Tempted? So you're not coming?"

"I'm afraid I can't make it today. I've got plans."

"Oh yeah? What's going on? Got a hot date?"

"Well… Yeah. I do."

"On a Thursday afternoon?"

She laughed. "Yep. I'm a rebel that way. I'd just left my place when you called. I'm walking to meet the guy now."

Padraig wasn't sure how to respond. In all the time he'd known Emmy, she'd never gone out on a date.

"That's great," he said lamely, when it was obvious she was waiting for him to say something.

"It's a first date. We're just meeting for coffee at Layla's shop."

"How did you meet him? Do I know him?"

"I doubt it. We met online."

"Online?"

"I signed up for one of those online dating apps."

Padraig *really* didn't know how to react to that. "Oh. Okay."

"I hate to cut this short, but I'm running a little late. I'll call you tomorrow and maybe we can do the pub tour then? I'm dying to see it, especially my spot."

"Sure. We'll do it tomorrow."

They said their goodbyes and hung up.

"Who was that?"

Padraig turned at the sound of Uncle Ewan's voice. "Emmy."

"How's she doing?"

"Good. She's doing good."

Ewan sighed. "I'll be damn glad when we get this place up and running again. It's hard not seeing everyone on a regular basis."

Padraig had heard that same complaint from pretty much every single member of his family since the fire. The Collins clan was a tight-knit group, most members always managing to stop by the pub two or three times a week to catch up on all the gossip. Without the pub, they'd been separated, sequestered in their own homes, something none of his nosy relatives were happy about.

"Why don't you invite her over?" Ewan gestured toward the bar. "Her seat is ready for her."

"I did," Padraig said. "She's got plans today. A date."

Ewan's eyebrows rose, mirroring the same astonishment Padraig felt when she'd announced that to him. "A date? With who? Do we know the guy?"

"She met him online. One of those dating apps," Padraig said, aware of the distinct grumble in his voice.

"Online dating?" Ewan said, not bothering to hide his disgust either. "Where's she meeting this guy? Somewhere public, I hope."

If there was one thing all the men in the Collins family had in common, it was their overprotectiveness when it came to the women in their lives.

"They're meeting for coffee at Layla's shop," Padraig replied.

"Well, that's good, I guess. Layla will keep an eye on her, and Finn and Fergus work right across the street. We can get them there quick if need be." Leave it to Ewan to pre-plan in case of attack.

Padraig felt his uncle studying his face when he didn't reply. If he hadn't been so blindsided by Emmy announcing she had a date, he might have managed to school his features.

As it was...

"You okay with her dating?" Ewan asked.

Padraig nodded, but it took him a few seconds to get his head bobbing. Those seconds were not missed by Ewan.

"You sure?" he stressed.

"I'm sure," Padraig said, hoping if he said the words out loud, he'd convince himself.

Ewan stared at him hard for a few moments more, then nodded. "Okay. Your dad just texted. He's on his way here now. When he arrives, how about we all sit down and start mapping out our next steps? I'd love to do a soft opening for family and friends next Friday."

"Sounds good."

An hour later, Padraig leaned against the counter, still waiting for the family powwow. His dad had arrived the same time as Joe Moretti, who'd warned them the big-screen TVs were on their way. The three of them had spent the past hour discussing whether or not to hang them in the same places as before or take advantage of this opportunity to put them in better locations. Now that the Morettis were in the physical process of putting them up, he, Dad, Keira, and Ewan could sit down to plan the reopening.

Aunt Keira walked up to him. "Ewan just got a call from the vendor who's printing the menus. He said once he's done, we can finally have our meeting. It feels like every time we cross one thing off our to-do list, another twenty-five things pop up on it."

"Yeah. It's been a lot," he agreed.

"Regardless, we're so close now, I can taste it," she said excitedly.

"We are." Padraig grinned, then turned at the sound of a knock on the front window.

He hurried to unlock the door when he saw Emmy waving at him through the large plate glass. He opened the door and his arms at the same time, chuckling when she stepped into them, giving him a huge hug.

"I missed you so much! You're not allowed to go away for that long again," she declared. "It sucked."

He tightened his grip when she started to let go, refusing to give her up just yet. He'd missed her as well.

And...she smelled good. Like apples and sunshine and summer.

When he finally released her, she gave him a curious look —just a brief one—before she glanced over his shoulder, her eyes widening. "Oh! Oh, Paddy. The pub...it's back."

She stepped around him, her gaze taking in everything that had taken his breath away when he'd first seen the place again as well.

"It's incredible," she gushed, spinning around slowly.

Then he watched as she walked to the mahogany bar, running her hand along it exactly as he had done earlier. She surreptitiously wiped away a tear as she looked at her nameplate.

"I can't believe how good it all looks," she whispered.

He walked next to her, wrapping his arm around her shoulder, feeling the need to touch her again. She looked up at him, that same questioning look in her eyes. Hugs were typically few and far between for them. Well, at least the ones initiated by him. Emmy was actually a big hugger and toucher, often bumping him with her shoulder or placing her hand on his arm as she told a story or laughed.

"I thought you had a date," he said.

She sighed heavily. "I did. It's already over."

Padraig looked at the time on his phone. "That was kind of quick, wasn't it?"

Emmy shrugged. "I think it was over about thirty seconds after it started. I'd messaged with the guy quite a few times, and he seemed really nice."

"So what happened?"

"I don't know. It sort of felt like he took one look at me

and…" She swallowed heavily, clearly uncomfortable as she added the last part. "Found me lacking."

Padraig scowled. "That's not possible. You're gorgeous."

She laughed softly, rolling her eyes in a way that proved she was dismissing his compliment. "You have to say that. You're my best friend."

"I'm saying it because it's true."

He wasn't sure he'd managed to convince her, but he couldn't call her out for it when she said, "Thanks."

"Sorry to interrupt. Oh, hi, Emmy," Joe said.

"Hey, Joey."

Joe narrowed his eyes, giving her a teasing look while pretending to be annoyed. "You spend too much time with my sister and cousin, otherwise, you'd know that's not my name."

Emmy lifted her shoulders. "Oops. I forgot. Joe," she corrected, drawing out that one syllable and dropping the y. Apparently everyone in the Moretti family refused to give up their "Joey," even though the man had insisted since graduating from high school that he wanted to use the more adult version of his name, preferring to be called just Joe.

Joe gave her a wink that was too fucking charming for Padraig's liking and said, "Atta girl."

"Did you need something?" Padraig asked.

"Yeah. We're going to have to pull more cable if we move that TV near the stage over to the left. Since it's only the difference of a few feet, I wondered if you thought it was worth the bother. I'm cool either way."

"It's not worth all that. The original place was fine. I know we'd prefer to have the TVs up and ready rather than slow the process."

"Yeah. That's what I thought." He turned to Emmy. "It was good to see you again, Emmy."

"You too, *Joe*," she replied with an adorable grin that was too flirty for Padraig's liking. It wasn't like it was the first time he'd seen a man flirt with her—or her flirt back—but this time...this time it bugged him.

Joe turned and walked away, and Padraig raised his eyebrows, giving her a knowing glance as she checked out the man's ass.

"Enjoying the show?" he muttered, aware she wasn't acting any differently than normal.

Nope. It was his reactions, his responses that were new.

She looked completely unremorseful. "Always."

"So the date was a bust?"

Emmy nodded. "Yeah. He obviously saw something he didn't care for."

"I might have a theory."

Padraig glanced over his shoulder when Aunt Keira spoke.

"I couldn't help overhearing," she said.

"Hi, Keira," Emmy said.

"Did you say you just came from a date?" his aunt asked.

Emmy nodded. "Yeah. I did."

"Were you wearing that?"

Padraig and Emmy both looked down at her outfit at the same time.

"Is something wrong with this?"

"Oh no, Emmy," Keira hastened to say. "It's just...well, you look like you're dressed for a job interview rather than a date."

Padraig studied what she was wearing but couldn't see anything wrong with it. She looked just as pretty as she always did.

Emmy sighed. "The man I was meeting owns his own business. In his profile pictures, he looked very professional, suit, tie, trendy haircut. I was trying to match that."

Keira grinned. "You look lovely but perhaps a bit too buttoned-up and stiff for a coffee date. I hope I'm not making you feel bad saying that."

"Oh no. You aren't at all."

"The truth is, I did the same thing on my first date with Will," Keira continued. "Although in my case, I borrowed a skirt and blouse from Teagan."

"Teagan?" Emmy asked. "But don't you two have very different tastes?"

Keira laughed. "Completely different. You should have seen Will's face when he saw me in that long, colorful, flowing skirt and peasant blouse. I looked like a rejected flower child from the sixties."

"I would have loved to see that," Emmy said, giggling.

"Obviously Will was confused. Even questioned me about it. When I admitted I didn't own a dress or skirt, he took me shopping on our second date. Helped me find something pretty that reflected who *I* was, not who Teagan was."

"That's so sweet," Emmy gushed. "I'm putting that in a book."

Keira was obviously amused and delighted, though not surprised. Emmy had made the "I'm putting that in a book" comment to pretty much every single person in his family at least once, and in some cases, multiple times. Because, according to his romance-writing friend, his family had the greatest love stories.

"I would love that. And if you do, I'm going to have to insist on knowing your pen name so I can buy it," Keira said.

"Deal," Emmy agreed.

"Are you sure it's so you can buy the book and not collect the pool money, Aunt Keira?" Padraig teased.

"I'll use my winnings to buy the book," Keira joked.

Emmy laughed. "I have serious concerns about the

gambling problem that seems to run rampant in the Collins family. I appreciate your comment about my outfit being inappropriate for a date. I'll admit I was equal parts mad and hurt when I thought the guy was judging me based solely on my looks."

Keira cupped Emmy's cheek with one hand. "Paddy's right. You are a lovely young woman. Inside and out. Never let any man's opinion make you feel otherwise."

Keira returned to Sunday's Side, leaving them alone again.

"Unlike Keira, I don't think I'm getting another chance to make a better second impression with that guy. Not that it matters. In addition to the fact he didn't care for my outfit, the conversation was pretty forced as well. It didn't help that the two of us were guzzling the steaming-hot coffee in an attempt to bring things to an end quickly. I burned the hell out of my tongue."

Padraig grinned, feeling ridiculously happy that her date had failed. Which made him a shitty friend. Not that he was going to chastise himself for that. "If it makes you feel any better, I'd definitely hire you if you showed up for an interview dressed like that."

Emmy playfully punched his arm. "Jerk." Then she said, "Next time, I'll invite Sunnie or Kelli over to help me pick an outfit."

"Next time?"

"Yeah." She took her phone out of her coat pocket. "Actually, I should probably text the girls now to see if they're available to help me sometime this weekend."

"This weekend?"

Emmy nodded. "I have a date next Wednesday—another rebellious dating day."

Padraig put his hand over her phone when she started

texting. "How many guys have you been talking to on this app?"

"A bunch," she admitted. "But I've narrowed it down to three I'd like to meet. And then there's the guy Caitlyn is setting me up with, who works with Lucas, and the fourth-grade teacher from Kelli's school."

"My cousin and sister-in-law are setting you up on blind dates?" Padraig asked, that knowledge feeling like a punch to the jaw for some reason.

"Yep," Emmy said. "And Layla offered me all four of her brothers, but I'm sure she was just joking." Emmy looked around him toward Joe and Tony, clearly taking delight in what she saw. "Well, pretty sure. More's the pity."

Padraig glanced in their direction, both men's muscles bulging as they hefted a large big-screen TV into the mounting bracket.

He thought back to Christmas Eve, to Emmy asking him out for a date. He'd come home from dinner at his parents' house and dropped down onto his couch, feeling lonely and wishing he'd invited Emmy to eat with them. As soon as the thought crossed his mind, he'd picked up his phone to call her, feeling better the second he'd heard her sweet, cheerful voice.

Then she'd asked him out on a date...and his gaze had landed on his Christmas tree, spotting the "Our First Christmas" ornament his mom had given him and Mia that included a photo of them with Seamus.

And he'd turned Emmy down...swallowing hard with the sudden awareness that he didn't really want to.

Now, he was being forced to acknowledge he'd locked Emmy in a box with a brass nameplate that said Reserved for Padraig Collins, even as he insisted on keeping her in that *just friends* column. He was terrified of...too fucking much when it came to her.

For a moment, he considered asking her out, but the words got lodged in his throat. Clearly he still wasn't ready. She deserved a shot at real happiness, and he was determined to help her find it.

"Don't text Sunnie or Kelli. I'll come over and help you pick out something to wear."

Emmy laughed as if he was joking.

When he didn't crack a smile, she sobered. "No offense, Paddy, but you didn't see anything wrong with *this* outfit."

"Regardless, I'm a guy, and I know what guys like. So I'm helping you."

"I...I'd prefer to ask the girls."

Padraig refused to take no for an answer. "I've missed you, Em. This will give us a chance to get together, to catch up."

She considered his response for long enough that he thought she'd stand by her rejection. He wasn't sure what to make of that. It wasn't unusual for them to hang out together at her place or his—either alone or with a bunch of his cousins.

Finally, she nodded. "Okay. Sure. Why don't you stop by Sunday around four? We can put together my," she finger-quoted, "*dating wardrobe*, then order pizza, and you can tell me all about your trip."

Padraig nodded, hoping she didn't catch his slight wince when he said, "It's a date," before he could think better of his words.

❦   3   ❦

"Thank God you're here," Emmy said as she opened the door to her apartment late Sunday afternoon.

Padraig stepped inside, took off his coat, and hung it on the old-fashioned coat rack standing by the entrance. "Why? What's wrong?"

"I stupidly thought I could start assembling a dating wardrobe on my own. So far, the only thing I've accomplished is destroying my bedroom."

He chuckled, then bent down to pick up Luna, who was weaving her way through his legs. "There's my sweet kitten."

She and Padraig had been amazed and amused when they discovered they'd managed to cover most of the minor Harry Potter characters when selecting names for their pets. She had Luna and Neville, her beloved cats, while Padraig was completely devoted to his adorable and extremely energetic dog, Seamus.

Luna purred in his arms, and Emmy started to lead the way toward her bedroom, but she detoured into the kitchen first. "Beer?"

"Sure."

She took out a bottle of Corona and held it up, laughing when he winced. "This is all I have."

He sighed as he put Luna down. "I guess I'll suffer through. Though after all the time we've spent together, you'd think you would have developed better taste in beer."

"Hey. I like Corona. Besides," she added, pulling out an open bottle of sauvignon blanc, "if given a choice, I'm always going to pour myself a glass of white wine."

She popped the top on Padraig's bottle of beer and handed it to him, laughing when he shook his head over her lack of limes, muttering, "amateur." Then she poured the wine for herself and the two of them continued down the hallway to her bedroom.

Padraig had been to her apartment countless times in the past couple of years, sometimes to hang out and watch movies, other times to help her fix various things. He'd spent the better part of a day back in November helping her fix a leaky pipe under her bathroom sink.

"Damn," he said, stepping into her room. "You weren't kidding about the destruction. Are there any clothes still hanging in the closet?"

"A few," she joked, walking over to her bed and picking up the short black skirt she'd found tucked in the back of her closet. "I'm afraid most of my clothes are yoga pants and T-shirts, the uniform of writers everywhere. But I did find this black skirt. I figure we could pair it with..." She looked at the mountains of clothes scattered around the room and shrugged. "Something."

Padraig set his beer down and started rummaging through her pile of tops until he found a hot-pink shirt she'd bought on a whim a few years back but never worn. "Why don't you ever wear this?" he asked, noticing it still had the tags on it.

"I didn't try it on in the store and when I got home, I discovered it was a little more lowcut than I realized. I was too lazy to return it."

Padraig grinned. "You had me at lowcut. Fashion show time. Put this on with the skirt." He walked over to her closet, crouching to look at her shoes. When he stood up, he had a pair of tall black boots in his hands. "I think these should work."

She had to agree. "Okay. Give me a minute to try it all together."

"Wait one second."

Emmy drew in a sharp breath when Padraig stepped in front of her and reached toward her face. For a second, she thought he was going to kiss her, but instead, he grasped the band she'd used to pull her hair into a messy bun and took it out. Her hair fell over her shoulders, and he ran his fingers through it, using them as a comb.

"Wear your hair down." His voice was gruff and soft and sexy.

Emmy licked her lips, quickly biting on the lower one in an attempt to hide her reaction to his hands in her hair. Padraig's gaze dropped to her lips, and she forgot to breathe until he took a step back. Then, he grabbed his beer, gave her a wink, and headed out of her bedroom. "I'll be in the living room."

"Shit," she whispered to herself once she was alone. She'd spent every second since Christmas trying to get her act together, and she thought she had.

Until now.

She was going to have to move across the country, maybe overseas, if she stood a chance of shaking free from these feelings for Padraig.

"You can do this," she muttered to herself, fluffing her hair as she gave herself a silent pep talk.

Just friends. Just friends. Just friends.

Once she managed to calm back down, Emmy undressed, then put on the outfit, slipping on the tall boots before looking in the mirror. She remembered once again why she'd never worn this shirt. Sticking her head out the door, she yelled down the hall. "This shirt is indecent. I think we need to find something else."

"Come out of there and let me see," he yelled back.

Emmy tugged at the neckline, but it did nothing to help. "I'm not sure—"

"Let me be the judge," he retorted, cutting her off.

She took a deep breath and walked down the hall, stepping into the living room.

Padraig's eyes widened as he wolf whistled, rising from the couch. "Holy shit, Em. You've got some seriously hot—" He stopped short, refraining from finishing his thought when she put her hands on her hips.

Regardless of what she'd intended to be an intimidating pose, his gaze traveled down the length of her body and back up again, stopping at her chest once more. When he lifted his eyes to hers, she sucked in a deep breath and internally yelled at herself for seeing something she knew wasn't there.

There was no way in hell Padraig was looking at her with such naked desire. She was misreading his expression, just like she had his actions in her bedroom.

Wishful thinking.

As always.

But when his expression didn't change, she struggled to find another way to describe it.

"I don't think—" she started.

"It's perfect. You look gorgeous. Sexy." Then his face

changed and this time, it was easy to read. He was scowling. "Actually, you might be right. Maybe we should find something a little less revealing."

"Nope. Too late, Dad," she teased. "You said gorgeous and sexy, so this is the outfit."

He looked like he wanted to continue to protest, but she merely raised one eyebrow, letting him know that argument would be pointless.

"So what's the plan for Wednesday's date? Another coffee meetup at Layla's shop?"

She shook her head. "Happy hour at a small bar near the waterfront with the guy Caitlyn's setting me up with. According to Lucas, he's nice, smart, funny, good-looking. I'm hoping this one goes better than the first."

Padraig nodded slowly. "You really think it was the outfit that messed up your date with that last guy?"

Emmy shrugged. "I don't know. I was thinking about it last night, and in truth, after I thought I saw that brief moment of disappointment in his eyes when we introduced ourselves, I dropped the ball on the rest. The conversation was awkward and uncomfortable. All we managed to cover was the weather—so lame—and what TV shows we liked to watch. And even those two topics felt like pulling teeth. Small talk is not my forte."

"You make small talk with me all the time," he said.

"Yeah, but you're easy to talk to. You have that master's degree in bartending that ensures you know all the right things to say."

"Yeah, that's me. A regular scholar." He chuckled at her jest. "Hey, you know what. Maybe we should practice."

"Practice?" she asked.

"Yeah. Let's pretend you and I are just meeting and this is

our first date. We can go through the whole thing, beginning to end."

Emmy thought that was the world's worst idea. She was barely managing to pretend she was okay with just being Padraig's friend. If he started acting like a would-be suitor, it would set her back at square one.

Then she grimaced.

Who was she fooling? She *was* still on square one.

"That's okay. I don't think—" She started to refuse.

"When's the last time you went on a date?"

"Four years ago."

Padraig's eyes widened in obvious surprise. "That's a long time. Who was the guy?"

"Someone my dad worked with. He set it up a few months after my mom died. Dad was concerned that I'd started to prefer the company of the characters in my books to that of real people. My teachers at school used to think I was shy, but I'm not uncomfortable around people. I just tend to live in my head a little bit too much sometimes. I think Dad was worried I'd disappear into myself and never come back out again."

"Well, we can't have that. I like having you out here in the real world with me too much. So order the pizza and I'll fill up our drinks," he said as he walked to the kitchen. "Then it's practice date time."

Emmy could tell he wasn't going to let her off the hook. He was determined to help her, his gesture very sweet and totally Padraig. He'd always been a good friend, and he'd never—not once—led her on or made her believe they could be more.

Nope. All those messed-up feelings were her fault, and hers alone.

"Fine," she said, firing up the app to order pizza.

"Though I'm telling you right now, I would never order pizza on a first date. Too messy, too greasy, and there's no sexy way to eat it."

"You could eat pizza, fried chicken, corn on the cob, hot dogs, or whatever other food you find unsexy in that shirt, and no man would complain. Ever," Padraig said as he popped the top on another beer and filled up her wineglass, even though she'd only taken a couple of sips. "Although, now that I think about it. Hot dogs, considering how you do it, aren't really—"

She smacked him on the arm before he could finish his joke. "Give me my wine, you pervert."

With dinner on the way, Padraig walked back into her living room, proclaiming it was now Emmy's Restaurant. Then he told her to go back to her bedroom and walk in again so they could start the pretend date from the very beginning.

She felt silly leaving and coming back. Until she reentered the room and Padraig looked at her with those dark brown eyes of his, his gaze taking in every inch of her again, and leaving her with that sense of being...desired.

"Hi," she said, holding out her hand. "I'm Emmy Martin."

"Padraig Collins," he said, taking her outstretched hand. "It's nice to meet you."

He gestured for her to sit. She started to claim the chair, leaving him the couch, but he still had a grip on her hand, so he used it to direct her to sit next to him. "Pretend it's a booth," he murmured.

"And we're sitting on the same side of it?" she asked incredulously.

"Stay in character, Em. So, tell me about yourself. What do you do for a living?"

"I'm a writer," she said. "Romance. And trust me, that is

not an invitation for you to send me a dick pic," she added with a laugh.

One Padraig didn't share. "Guys are sending those to you?" There was no mistaking from the angry tone that he was no longer playing the game.

She shrugged. "A few. And I obviously blocked them on the app after that. I was just joking around, Paddy. It's not a big deal."

"I'm not sure this online dating is a good idea. Might not be safe."

She rolled her eyes. "It's fine. I block the creeps, message with the nice ones for a few weeks to feel them out, and I'm only setting up dates where I meet the men in public."

"After Wednesday's date, why don't you wait until the pub reopens before you go on any more. You can meet the guys there where I can keep an eye on you."

She shook her head. "Hell no! I don't even want to think about you, your dad, your uncles, and your Pop Pop hovering around, giving my date the evil eye. I've heard the horror stories from Sunnie and Darcy, so I know how you all are."

"You need someone to look after you since your brother isn't around."

Emmy snorted. "Sam wasn't around enough for us to ever get very close, and I would never use the word overprotective to describe him. Though one time, he...he came through for me."

"What's that mean?"

Emmy hadn't told anyone about the last time she'd seen her brother, mainly because at the time, there hadn't been anyone to tell.

And then, after enough time passed, she didn't want to think about it again.

"He moved back in here after my dad died."

"I didn't know that," Padraig said.

"He didn't stay long. Only a month or so. Said with our parents dead, it fell to him to look after me. I pointed out I was twenty-four and not a kid, but he insisted."

"Why did he leave after a month if he wanted to protect you?"

"I'm getting there. Sam had been crashing at a friend's house before moving back. The last time he'd been home when my dad was alive, he'd stolen a bunch of stuff to sell for drug money. My dad had kicked him out and told him not to come back until he was clean. I know that sounds bad, but the truth is, my dad had tried a hundred different ways to help my brother, but...Sam has always been his own worst enemy."

"I don't think your dad was wrong to kick him out. You know what they say about having to hit rock bottom."

"Sam hadn't hit it when he moved back in. He only came back because Dad was gone. So, you know, free place to stay, free rein to steal stuff. I hid everything of value, everything I cared about, in my bedroom, and put a lock on the door. Sam's friends started coming by, getting stoned, drunk, basically trashing the place. I stayed in my room, sneaking out for food whenever they left or passed out."

"Jesus," Padraig muttered.

"One night, I woke up to a loud crash. One of Sam's friends had kicked in my bedroom door."

"Fuck." Padraig shifted closer, his expression so fierce, she felt a tremor of fear, even though she knew it wasn't directed at her. "What did he do to you?"

"Nothing. He never laid a finger on me."

"What?" Padraig asked, unconvinced.

"He was walking toward my bed, but before I had time to reach for something to use as a weapon or scream, Sam was there. He pulled the guy out of the room and pummeled him. Then he kicked him—and everyone else—out of the apartment. The next morning, Sam was sitting on the couch when I came out of my room. Said he was leaving. And he was sorry."

Padraig reached for her, and she accepted—needed—his hug. A lot of the guilt her father had felt in regards to Sam had transferred to her after his death, and she'd spent more than a few sleepless nights wondering if there had been some way to reach him, to help him.

She gone to visit him in jail shortly after his arrest—intent on bailing him out—but he'd refused the money and to see her. Sent word through his state-appointed attorney that he wouldn't accept the bail and that she was better off without him in her life.

She'd refused to accept that, so she started writing him letters after his conviction, and after a year or so, he'd finally relented and agreed to start taking her occasional phone calls. Emmy still hoped that eventually he would let her visit him at the prison in person.

"I'm glad he protected you, but I'm still going to kick his ass when he gets out of jail for putting you in danger in the first place."

Emmy started to pull back. Padraig tightened his grip, just as he'd done at the pub on Thursday. The self-sabotaging part of her decided to think it was because he didn't want to let her go. In reality, he probably thought she needed the extra bit of comfort.

"You'll have to wait three more years, two if he behaves himself," she said, lifting her head, trying to lighten the moment.

"I wish I'd known you then."

"Me too." Suddenly she became aware of how close they

were, their faces just inches apart. She cleared her throat, putting some distance between them, lest she lose her mind and do something insane.

Like kiss him.

"We're getting off track," she said, reminding him of their practice date.

"You're right. Sorry about that. Strangers again," he said with an endearing grin. He took a moment and then said, "So what made you decide to become a romance writer, Emmy?"

She grinned. "That's easy. My parents."

"How so?" he asked curiously.

There were two subjects she and Padraig had never really delved into.

Mia and her parents.

Every time those subjects came up, they managed to keep the conversation factual and surface-y.

She knew how Mia died, and she'd picked up a million tiny details about Padraig's beloved wife, simply through eavesdropping on his conversations with his family.

And he knew how her parents died as well. But she'd never really talked about them to him, just as he'd never really discussed Mia.

When they'd first met, they'd both been grieving and unwilling to share that pain.

But now...for the first time, it felt as if enough time had passed that she wanted Padraig to know about them. To *really* know about them.

"My mom was the greatest storyteller ever. She had this huge, vivid imagination and a way of creating these make-believe worlds that felt real. For the first eight years of my life, I was convinced we shared this apartment with a town full of nocturnal fairies who lived under the furniture and only came out at night when we were asleep."

Padraig chuckled. "Fairies, huh?"

"Yeah. Every now and then, I still say hello to Hungry Harry, the chubby fairy who lives in a condo behind the refrigerator. I don't doubt for a minute that it's him who steals all the cookies because they seem to vanish quicker than they should. I mean, I know it's not me eating them."

He reached out and ruffled her hair playfully. "I've seen you when Aunt Riley brings out a tray of her homemade chocolate chip cookies at parties. No one—fairy or otherwise—would get between you and that platter."

Emmy didn't bother to deny her sweets addiction. "Your Pop Pop reminds me of my mom. He has that same talent for weaving tales, for drawing pictures in your mind of times long past. I think that's why I've always been so drawn to him. Because of his stories about Sunday and your aunts and uncles when they were younger, as well as the ones about you, your cousins, your brother. Colm sounds like he was a bit of a handful."

"Still is," Padraig agreed. "Pop Pop *is* a great storyteller. So you got your romance writing skills from your mom."

Emmy shook her head. "Nope. Got the storytelling from my mom. The romance part was all my dad. He was, quite simply, the most romantic man I've ever known."

Padraig considered that for a moment. "Is that right? How so?"

"He was super sweet and really thoughtful. He worked long hours. Like ten- to twelve-hour shifts, six, sometimes seven days a week. But every single day, he'd come home with some small gift for me and my mom. Flowers, candy, sticks we could use to make Harry Potter wands, or even rocks."

"Rocks?"

Emmy stood up and crossed to the pile of rocks in a small

dish on her bookshelf. "You never wondered what these were?"

Padraig nodded. "Actually I did, but I thought maybe they were just some kind of girly decoration I didn't understand."

Emmy laughed. "No. They were gifts from my dad. He would come home with a rock that caught his eye, either because of its color or shape. He'd give it to us, and then my mom would tell us the story of the rock." She picked one up. "This one has magical properties. And this one," she said, lifting up a second, "traveled all over the world in the pocket of a great adventurer. You couldn't believe all the things it's seen."

Padraig stood and picked up a third. "And this one?"

"Was once a handsome prince but is now suffering from a curse cast by an evil witch. I'm sad to say he's destined to remain a rock until his princess finds him and frees him with a kiss."

"How many times have you kissed the rock?" Padraig asked with a grin.

"When I was younger, about a million times. I really wanted to be that princess." Emmy looked at the rocks. "I remember every single rock's story. And I keep them because someday I'm going to tell the stories to my own kids."

"They're going to love these rocks. Where was your brother when all of this was happening?"

"Sometimes he was here and he heard the stories, shared the sweets. He even made a wand with us once, and the two of us cast spells on each other all night. I always liked it when he was with us. But most of the time, he wasn't. Especially as I got older. My brother was sort of an oopsie baby. My mom got pregnant when she was dating my dad, so they got married. Although they both insisted they were headed to the altar regardless. They were young and poor and barely making ends meet. My brother was nearly seven when they had me. By then, their lives were more settled. Because he was so much older, there were times when I felt like an only child. He fell in with a bad crowd at thirteen. I'm pretty sure that's when the drugs started. My dad blamed himself, his long work hours, for Sam drifting so far away from us."

"And your mom?"

"She couldn't control him. He was always angry, and my mom, well, I'm not sure I ever saw her mad a day in her life. She was a very gentle soul."

"You take after her then."

Emmy gave him a curious look.

"I've never seen you lose your temper either."

Emmy was touched to be compared to her beloved mother. "Plus, she couldn't have helped him after..." Emmy swallowed down the lump in her throat. "She was diagnosed with ALS when I was seventeen—I told you that, right?"

Padraig nodded. "You did."

"After that, she was too sick to be much help with Sam. I dropped out of school and—"

"You dropped out of school?"

Emmy didn't tell many people that fact. "I got my GED. My dad needed to work for the health insurance, so I stayed home to take care of my mom and the apartment. That was when I started writing. She'd spent my entire life telling me stories, so I figured it was my turn. I wrote whenever she was asleep, and when she woke up, I'd read what I'd written, to her. She loved romance novels, so that was what I wrote. Although, those earlier stories were much less steamy...closed bedroom door and all that."

"I think that's the nicest thing I've ever heard."

She gave him a look that screamed "really?" "I've heard of

nicer things, Paddy. Maybe take a look in the mirror and think about it a minute or two."

After all, Padraig spent a year helping Mia accomplish everything on her bucket list after he discovered she was dying of a brain tumor.

He rolled his eyes at her, amused.

"My mom was my best friend," she continued. "After she died, I sort of disappeared for a little while. Spent every waking hour writing stories because it was easier to live in my fictional worlds than in the real one. A world without my mom wasn't one I wanted to be in. Dad put his foot down, determined I wasn't going to hide inside for the rest of my life. So he set me up with a guy, Tim, from his work. And I went out with him to make Dad happy because I knew he was as devastated as I was over Mom's death, and I wanted to set his mind at ease...at least over me. He had enough to deal with, grieving over Mom, worrying about Sam. I never wanted to add to his stress."

Padraig ran his hand over her cheek tenderly, and it took a moment for Emmy to recover from the sweet touch to continue her story.

"Anyway, Tim was a really nice guy and we had a good time together, but I think we both knew we weren't suited to each other for the long run. But the dates with him helped because they got me out of the apartment, got me living again. Then Dad had a massive heart attack a year after Mom died and...it set me back for a little while. Of course, all that shit with Sam didn't help either."

Padraig was quiet for a few minutes. Then he asked the question she'd been expecting. "Why didn't I know any of this, Em?" he asked, genuinely curious. "About your parents, your brother?"

"Because for a long time, it hurt to talk about them. I miss them every day. And also, because you—" She stopped herself before offering the other reason.

Not that it mattered.

Sometimes it felt like Padraig could read her mind. "Because I was grieving too."

She nodded slowly. "You've never really talked to me... about her."

"You're right. I haven't. I..." He looked down at her rocks again. "I'd like to. If you wouldn't mind listening."

She reached out and took his hand, giving it a gentle squeeze. "I'm a sucker for a good love story."

✳︎   4   ✳︎

adraig leaned back and looked at the clock, suddenly aware they'd been talking for close to three hours. They'd polished off a large supreme pizza while he'd drunk five Coronas and she'd finished her bottle of wine.

Once he'd started, it was as if the floodgate had opened and he found himself telling Emmy things he'd never told anyone about Mia. About how she could cook wonderful meals but burned every single thing she ever tried to bake. How she'd become addicted to *The Young and the Restless* after she was too sick to work. The way he'd felt as he held her in his arms when they stood together at Sacre Coeur, how he'd wanted to freeze time, right there in that moment, forever.

"So you seriously told your dad you were marrying Mia after talking to her just one night?" Emmy asked.

Padraig nodded. "Yeah. Needless to say, he was very confused."

"I don't know," she mused. "I've seen your dad with your mom. He's very protective, devoted. Your mom told me once that she was married before your dad, that her ex-husband was a violent man."

Padraig scowled, the idea of his mother's ex always prompting that response. "He was an abusive asshole. Put her in the hospital the night she tried to leave him. Then he actually kidnapped her."

"And your dad risked his life to save her."

Padraig and Colm had been adults the first time they'd heard the horrifying story of their mother's abduction and the rescue attempt staged by their dad, Ewan, and Aaron. "He did."

"You and your dad seem to have very similar personalities, always there to protect, to help, to defend. I have a feeling he understood your need to marry Mia, even if he didn't agree right away."

Padraig considered that, then thought she was probably right. "I was alone with her the night she died. My parents, Pop Pop, and Colm had been there off and on throughout the day. We knew it was just a matter of time, and they'd wanted to stay close. But as it got later and later, I insisted that they go home."

Emmy reached out and took his hand. He squeezed it gently, touched by her comforting gesture.

"It was the middle of the night and her breathing...well... there's this sound..."

"Death rattle," Emmy whispered. "I heard it...with my mom."

Padraig shifted closer to her on the couch, wrapping his free arm around her shoulders while retaining his grip on her other hand. "Her breathing was the only sound in the apartment. I crawled into the hospital bed with her, lying on the edge, facing her. I was holding her hand," he continued, looking at their linked fingers. "Running my thumb over the top, back and forth. I whispered that I loved her. I'd said it to her countless times that day, hoping, praying she could hear me. But that time…I told her it was okay for her to go." He mimicked the stroking motion on Emmy's hand. "There was a light on in the hallway, so while the room was dim, I could still see her face. She'd been asleep the entire day, but I felt her hand stir and when I looked, her eyes were open. She smiled at me—just one small, sweet, perfect smile—then she closed her eyes again. And then…it was quiet. Absolutely silent."

Emmy tried to discreetly wipe away the tears in her eyes. Padraig pulled her close, holding her as she cried—for him? For Mia?

He hadn't thought about that night in months. And he'd never told anyone about it. The memory didn't gut him like it did during that first year after she passed, when it was the only thing he saw every night when he closed his eyes.

"She was lucky to have you," Emmy said once she'd managed to pull herself together.

"I was the lucky one."

Emmy smiled at that. "I think I might have to revise my previous statement. You *and* my dad are the most romantic men I've ever known."

"I don't know about that. I've never given a woman a rock," he said, grateful for the opportunity to lighten the heaviness that had fallen between them.

"Maybe you will one day. And she'll fall head over heels in love with you because what woman can resist a rock," she teased. Then she glanced down at herself. "I probably should have changed out of this outfit. At least I didn't get any pepperoni grease on my shirt."

He reached out with this free hand and flipped one side of her long blonde hair over her shoulder, feeling the need to touch it again. It was soft, silky, beautiful. Like her. "Remember to leave your hair down for the date."

She smiled, her cheeks flushing slightly. "I will. No more button-up job interview outfits for me."

"I'm not sure I helped you much with the small-talk issue, considering I did most of the talking. Our practice session went off the rails. Completely."

"That's okay. I'll google first date topics tomorrow."

"When are you going to tell me your pen name, Em?" he asked, suddenly curious.

Her response—as always—was quick and succinct. "Never."

"Chicken shit," he teased.

"Why are you asking me that right now?"

He shrugged. "I'm curious how you can write romance when you claim to be a dating disaster."

"I just told you that my parents had a loving relationship. I mean, it was the real deal. And I'm also an avid reader."

He tilted his head. "What does reading have to do with it?"

She rolled her eyes. "Spoken like someone who thinks flipping through *Sports Illustrated* counts as reading."

He chuckled. "Wait. That's not reading? Because I promise you, I pore over that swimsuit issue."

"How am I friends with you?" she asked laughing. "All I'm saying is you don't actually have to date to fall in love. I have fallen madly in love with some of the hottest fictional heroes out there."

"Like?" he prompted, amused by this whole concept.

"I've had torrid affairs with Jamie Fraser, Ian Taggart, and Eric Ericsson.

Padraig laughed. "Should I be jealous?"

"Absolutely," she answered without hesitation. He noticed the second she paused and tilted her head curiously.

Why would he be jealous?

He could almost read the question in her eyes.

And she'd be right to feel confused.

If they were just friends, why *would* he be jealous?

"We're doing a soft reopening of the pub on Friday," he said, grasping for anything that might distract her from his faux pas. If that's what it was.

Her eyes widened. "And I'm just hearing about it? Wait. What does 'soft opening' mean?"

"Friends and family only. Gives us a chance to test out all the new stuff. The equipment in the kitchen, the beer taps, the bathrooms. Invite only."

She gave him a look. "Okay. I'm waitttting..." she singsonged.

He laughed. "You're invited. That should go without saying. My dad, Ewan, Pop Pop, Riley, Yvonne, and at least six other relatives all checked with me to make sure I'd told you to come."

"I wouldn't miss it for the world!" She leaned in and hugged him, her excitement contagious.

"Good." Unlike the last two times he'd hugged her, he kept this embrace short, friendly. It felt as if he was straddling a line right now, friendship on one side and...something else on the other.

The fact that he couldn't name the *something else* seemed to indicate he still wasn't ready. Right?

He'd just spent the entire evening talking about Mia, and he would have expected that sharing those memories would push him solidly back on the "just friends" side.

But it hadn't. It actually felt as if it had drawn him closer to...something else.

Shit.

Nothing was happening between them tonight. Not until he got his damn head screwed on straight.

Emmy, oblivious to the internal war raging inside him, stood and picked up the empty pizza box and paper plates. He grabbed his empty beer bottles and her wineglass and followed her to the kitchen. They tidied up for a few minutes, then she walked with him to the door.

The night certainly hadn't gone the way he'd expected. He'd come here intent on helping her find a way to navigate the murky waters of dating. He wanted her to be happy, wanted that more than he could say. And if reentering the dating world was what she wanted, then he wanted it for her.

But instead of him coaching her, she'd sat down on that couch beside him and...given him exactly what he needed. A chance to talk out so many things he'd kept bottled up inside for years.

They shared a bond—grieving those they'd lost—and he'd never felt closer to her than he did in this moment.

"Thanks for tonight, Paddy. I've missed you the last couple of months, since the fire and the trip."

He nodded, trying to return the friendly smile she was giving him, but he couldn't do it. That "something else" was dragging him over the line into uncharted territory again.

If he was a good friend, he'd thank her for the beer, the pizza, the conversation, and he'd walk out.

"I might be a lousy small-talk coach, but there's one thing I can help you with," he said.

"What's that?"

He reached out and cupped her cheeks. "The good-night kiss."

"Paddy..." she started.

If she intended to say something else, he didn't give her the chance. He couldn't.

He lowered his head, his lips finding hers.

He kept the kiss gentle, an exploration, a soft stroking, more glancing touches than true kisses. Emmy didn't try to pull away. Instead, she lifted her hands to his shoulders, resting them there lightly as if waiting to see where he was going to take them next.

He turned his head slightly to deepen the kiss, pushing her lips open with his, tongue searching for hers. She met him halfway, their breath mingling. He slowly built the kiss, twisting their bodies as he did so, until Emmy's back was pressed against the door.

He pushed closer, needing to feel more than just her soft lips. His chest was tight against her breasts, his legs tangled with hers, his left thigh shifting ever closer to her pussy.

Emmy lifted her hands from his shoulders, gripping his hair almost desperately, using the grasp to keep his lips on hers, her breaths coming more rapidly.

His hands drifted from her cheeks to the sides of her neck, his thumb brushing the pulse point there.

Her heart was racing. So was his.

She rotated her hips, just slightly. An invitation for him to rub his thigh against her more firmly. She gasped when he applied pressure just where she needed it most.

A growl rumbled low in his throat when she tried to turn her head to suck in some much-needed air. "Paddy," she said, breathlessly.

He wasn't finished with the kiss. Not by a long shot.

He twisted her face back to his and kissed her again. All traces of gentleness were gone now. This kiss was rough, demanding.

Jesus. Padraig had never kissed a woman like this before.

It was passion, hunger, desire. Agony.

That was when he realized Emmy's hands were back on his shoulders. Only this time, she was pushing him away.

Padraig broke off the kiss and—while it wasn't easy—forced himself to take a step away.

"Em," he whispered, awareness dawning slowly. "I didn't mean—"

"I know," she interrupted, her smile sweet but sad. "That's why I stopped. It makes sense, Paddy. After all, we spent the whole night talking about Mia. I'm sure it brought up some feelings...maybe loneliness?" she suggested. "And you reached out."

She thought he'd kissed her because he missed Mia?

He'd intended to say he hadn't meant to be so rough.

Before he could correct her, she continued, "I'm glad I could be here for you, but I don't think...we can't let it go any further. I mean, I don't...I can't..."

He watched as she fought for the words to say what she was thinking. He was having the same problem himself, struggling to explain his actions, his feelings.

He was reeling from that kiss.

Finally, he let them both off the hook. "It's okay, Emmy. I let that go way too far, too fast. Maybe we should take a big step back from this." He started to add, "for now," but stopped himself.

She nodded, clearly relieved he was giving her a reprieve. "I'll see you at the soft opening on Friday," she said.

He didn't like the idea of not seeing her for nearly a week, but given the current cyclone of emotions ravaging his insides, it was probably a good idea for him to take some time to figure his shit out.

"See you Friday." He left, listening as she locked the door

to her apartment, then he walked down the two flights of stairs and out into the chilly night.

Tugging his coat around him to ward off the frigid February wind, Padraig walked to his apartment, trying to wrap his head around what he'd just done. What he'd felt.

He hadn't kissed a woman since Mia. And he hadn't expected it to—fuck—affect him like that. One touch and it was as if he'd lost all sense of time and place. And there was no question in his mind that if she hadn't pushed him away, he would have dragged her back to her bedroom, tossed her down on that mountain of clothes, and...

And what?

He would have had sex with Emmy.

He stopped in the middle of the sidewalk as he let that idea play out.

He would have slept with her.

As that reality sank in, he waited for it. The guilt, the pain, the confusion. Any of that. Maybe all of it.

It didn't come.

What the fuck did that mean?

He reached into his coat pocket and pulled out his phone. Colm answered on the third ring.

"What's up, bro?" Colm asked.

Padraig didn't mince words. He didn't have to with his twin. "I kissed Emmy tonight."

"Good for you."

Padraig snorted and rolled his eyes. "That's it? That's all you've got for me?"

"What do you *want* me to say, Paddy?" Colm asked. "Because if you're looking for someone to chastise you or tell you it was a mistake, you called the wrong number."

He swallowed hard and said the one thing that kept coming

back to him. "I...I didn't think about her." That was the part that was the most shocking to him. The entire time he was kissing Emmy, she was all he could see, smell, taste, think of.

He'd expected Mia to be there, always in the back of his mind. But she'd been absent.

Once again, Colm didn't need clarification. Sometimes it seemed as if they shared a hive mind. "That's good. Progress. Means you're ready to move on."

Then Padraig heard Kelli's voice in the background, and Colm said, "He kissed Emmy." That was followed up with, "Dammit, Kell! I'm talking," before Colm said, "fine. Here."

"Paddy." Kelli's voice came through the phone, and he grinned. Before Emmy came along, Kelli had been his best friend, the one he told everything. Then his brother opened his eyes and realized Kelli was actually the woman of his dreams. Since then, Kelli had become something so much better than a friend. Padraig now had a sister. One he adored and loved.

"Hey, Kell."

"So you finally pulled your head out of your ass. 'Bout damn time."

Padraig started to reconsider the adore part. "She's joined one of those online dating things."

"I know."

Padraig approached the front of his building but hesitated before going in. "She has a date this week."

"I know that too. And you're going to resist the alpha male voice in your head that's screaming she's yours and let her go on that date."

Padraig was surprised by Kelli's insistence. "Kelli, I—" he started.

"She doesn't have a lot of dating experience."

"Yeah. I sort of figured that out."

Kelli huffed as if that should explain something—anything —to him. "You need to let her go on that date because it will show her what those of us who spent way too long in the playing-the-field pool already know. Dating sucks."

"What if she likes the guy?"

While he couldn't see her face, he could hear the eye roll in her voice. "Did she kiss you back?"

"Yeah."

"She's crazy about you, Paddy. Remember, you were the first guy she asked out back before Christmas. And like a dumbass, you turned her down and said you couldn't be more than just friends."

He frowned. "That was a mistake."

"Of course it was. But the fact is, *you* were her first choice. And after a couple of awkward dates with strangers, she's going to figure out you're also her only choice."

"So I shouldn't go back to her place tonight?"

"Absolutely not. You're thinking with your dick right now. Give your other head a chance to catch up. Because Emmy's not the only one who needs some time and space to come to grips with what's finally happening. Let the dust settle on the kiss."

Kelli was right. He was acting on impulse, still turned on from that kiss. "Okay. You're right."

"Music to my ears. Wish I'd had the phone on speaker so Colm could've heard you say that."

Padraig chuckled.

"Besides," Kelli continued, "you're going to be wicked slammed this week, working to get the pub ready for Friday. Even if you wanted to get things rolling with Emmy, this wouldn't be the time to do it. Give her a week to think about that hot kiss—please tell me it was a hot kiss," she begged.

"It was hot. Scorching." Even now, his lips burned from the memory of it.

"Awesome. So she'll be remembering that while living through what's certain to be another lackluster date. On Friday, she can take her place at the end of the counter and the two of you can fall madly in love, get married, and make lots of babies who will be best-friend cousins to my twins."

Padraig chuckled. "Got it all planned, do you?"

"I have spoken. It is so."

"Love you, Kell," he said. Then he heard Colm curse in the background, loudly asking, "What in the hell are you feeding these kids?"

"Jesus H., Colm. You graduated top of your class in law school, for God's sake. Take a deep breath and change the shitty diaper. It's not rocket science," Kelli yelled back. "Still coming over for dinner and to watch hockey tomorrow, Paddy?"

"Yep."

"See you then."

Before she clicked end, he could hear Colm declaring, "This smell is ungodly. I'm gonna puke."

Padraig laughed as he climbed the stairs to his apartment, Kelli's words giving him hope.

And something he hadn't experienced in a long time.

Something to look forward to.

Friday.

5

It was Friday night, and Emmy looked at her reflection in the mirror for the hundredth time in an hour, chastising herself for doing so. Regardless, she couldn't make herself stop doing it because every time she looked, she found fault with something else, be it her earrings, shade of lipstick, or that one piece of hair on the right side that just wouldn't lay right.

She forced herself out of the bathroom, muttering to herself, "It's just a date. Just a date."

A date with Joe Moretti.

She'd been shocked when he'd called her this morning to ask if she wanted to attend the soft opening of Pat's Pub with him tonight.

She'd said yes before her brain kicked in and she realized exactly what she was agreeing to.

For one thing, according to his sister, Layla, Joe was the ultimate bad boy and the only one of her brothers she swore she'd never set a friend up with. Simply because he was king of the charming heartbreakers.

Emmy's dating skills still had training wheels, so going out with Joe felt like the equivalent of tossing her bicycle into the grass, hopping aboard a Harley, and hitting the open highway.

And if that wasn't enough, the other—and main—reason was Padraig was going to be at the pub tonight. She was still reeling from that "practice" good-night kiss of his last Sunday. So much so, she'd screwed up the date with Brian, the guy from Lucas's work, on Wednesday night.

Well, screwed up was probably the wrong description. She'd shown up at the bar and tried to make some sort of connection with the man. He was actually really nice, but she'd spent the entire date comparing everything he said and did to Padraig and found him lacking right down the line. He'd ordered a Corona, proclaiming it his favorite beer, then he'd admitted to never reading Harry Potter or seeing one of the movies, and finally he threw her for a loop when he said he wasn't a fan of cats. And it wasn't because of allergies, because that she could at least understand and forgive. When she asked about dogs, he clarified, saying he wasn't a pet person.

Who the hell wasn't a pet person?

So, the happy-hour date had ended just as quickly and awkwardly as the coffee date. And to add insult to injury, Padraig texted her that night to see how things had gone. It had been hard to admit she'd failed yet again.

The worst part was, she couldn't read the tone in his response when he'd asked about the good-night kiss, and she told him the date had ended with a handshake at the exit of the bar.

All he'd said was "good."

What the hell did that mean?

Whether he realized it or not, Padraig was giving her

some seriously mixed-up signals, and it was screwing with her head...and her heart.

At least going with Joe to the soft opening of the pub tonight should make Padraig happy. He'd told her to start bringing her dates to the pub so he could keep an eye on her. She was hoping the fact she was with one of the Moretti brothers would be a point in her favor, since every member of the Collins family had done nothing but sing their praises the last two months.

She hadn't seen the final results of their efforts on the pub, but Sunnie had called yesterday and declared it was all perfect and the Morettis were nothing short of genius.

Emmy was pulled from her thoughts by a knock at the door.

She took a deep breath to steady herself.

"Well," she murmured. "Here goes nothing."

She pulled it open and smiled when Joe Moretti said, "Hello there, gorgeous."

Emmy took the hand he proffered, suddenly certain that tonight's date was going to be a good one.

Finally.

Padraig grinned when his grandfather bellied up to the bar in his usual spot.

"I'd like a pint of Guinness, my boy," Pop Pop said with a huge smile on his face.

Padraig reached for one of the shiny, new pint glasses, emblazoned with the Pat's Pub logo, and filled it from the tap. "Your first beer in the new and improved pub," he said, sliding the glass across the counter.

Pop Pop lifted it in a silent toast and then took a long swig. "Ahhhh. Best beer I've ever had."

Padraig grabbed a second glass, filling it with just a few sips of their Irish champagne, then tapped his pint against Pop Pop's. "We're back," he said softly.

Pop Pop grinned. "I never doubted it for a minute." Then he glanced down the bar at Emmy's empty seat. "Where's our girl?"

Padraig liked the way Pop Pop referred to Emmy as theirs. His beloved grandfather had claimed Emmy as his own since the day she first walked into the pub, referring to her as "my girl" initially. Somewhere over the past six months or so, Padraig noticed the pronoun had turned from "my" to "our."

"She'll be here," Padraig reassured him. "I invited her Sunday night. And confirmed last night by text."

"I was pleased to see Gio remembered to include our reserved nameplates," Pop Pop said, running his finger along his name before picking up a napkin to wipe away the smudge he'd left behind.

"The nameplates were the first thing I mentioned when we talked about the design for the rebuild. Couldn't have anyone sitting in yours or Emmy's spot."

Pop Pop ran his hand over the smooth countertop, a gesture Padraig had repeated himself more times than he could count. He swallowed heavily when he saw a tear in his grandfather's eye.

"I didn't expect it to be so perfect...didn't dare to hope..." Pop Pop's smile was wide when he said, "We got our pub back, Paddy."

Padraig, unable to speak past the lump in his throat, merely reached over to pat Pop Pop's hand and nod.

"Feels like coming home after years away," Pop Pop added.

"Goddammit," his father, Tris, muttered from behind him.

"Language," Pop Pop said with a chuckle, and just like that, the emotional moment lightened.

"Sorry, Pop," Tris replied by rote.

It was a standard interchange between Pop Pop and basically every single member of the family, all of them big fans of cursing. The offender would swear, Pop Pop would utter that lone word, and the apology would follow. His grandfather's continual admonitions never had a lasting effect. Pretty much every member of the Collins family—with the exception of Pop Pop—cussed like a sailor.

"Something wonky is going on with the Bud tap, Paddy," Dad said. "Bend down there and see if it's connected right."

Padraig squatted down to check. "Oh yeah. One of the tubes came loose. Hang on a second." He reached back to reconnect it.

He was just rising when he heard his father say, "Fuck."

Padraig glanced back down to make sure he hadn't screwed something else up, but everything looked fine.

That's when he realized Pop Pop didn't say "language."

Instead, what his grandfather said was much worse.

"Shit."

Padraig stood up.

"What's wrong?" he asked, but his father and grandfather were both looking toward the front entrance.

He turned just in time to see Joe Moretti and Emmy walk in together.

Joe took her coat, hanging it on a hook near the door, then placed his hand on her back to guide her farther into the pub.

Padraig saw red, clenching his jaw so tightly, he was surprised his teeth weren't shattering. There was no way he was seeing what he thought he was seeing.

Joe and Emmy made their way over to the bar. She stepped up next to Pop Pop and gave him a hug.

"Welcome back, Mr. Collins. Paddy told me a bit about your

trip. Sounds like it was amazing," she said. "You and I are going to have to make a lunch date one day soon so I can hear all about it."

"My dear Emmy, I've told you a million times to call me Pat. And it was a brilliant trip, lass. A one-in-a-million opportunity. I'm going to hold you to those lunch plans."

"This place," she said, looking around, her voice filled with awe.

"I know," Pop Pop said. "Paddy and I were just remarking on it." He looked over her shoulder at Joe. "You and your brothers do fine work, Joe. Very fine indeed."

Joe nodded. "Thank you, Mr. Collins. That means a lot to me."

Under normal circumstances, Padraig would have joined the conversation, but at the moment, he was too fixated on Joe's hand, on the way it had returned to the small of Emmy's back after she'd hugged his grandfather.

"Hey, Joe!"

Their small group looked over to see Tony waving to his brother. Joe looked at Emmy. "I'm going to go say hello to my brothers, then grab us a booth."

"Cool," she said. "I'll order our drinks. What would you like?"

"Peroni would be great." Joe turned to walk away as Padraig scoffed.

"Peroni," he said with disgust.

Emmy laughed and teasingly called him a beer snob.

"You're here on a date with Joe Moretti?" Padraig asked as he poured Joe's beer, then reached for the bottle of Emmy's favorite Chardonnay.

"Yes. Do you believe it?" she said, giving him a wide-eyed look, mouthing OMG. The response would have been adorable if Padraig wasn't so...pissed off. "He called me this morning to see if I was coming tonight. When I said yes, he asked if I wanted to go with him. Since you told me to start bringing my dates here, I figured you'd be pleased."

Padraig could feel the weight of his father's and grandfather's stares as they both looked in his direction. Their expressions, if he'd bothered to glance their way, would no doubt be of the WTF variety.

Emmy picked up their drinks from the counter as he pushed them across to her and said "thanks" before turning to find Joe.

Padraig watched as she slid into the curved corner booth next to Joe, who wasted no time resting his arm on the back of the seat behind her. If the man got any more handsy, tonight was going to end in a brawl.

Finn and Layla walked up to the bar, both of them looking back to where Joe and Emmy sat.

"Did Emmy just walk in here with Joe?" Finn asked.

Padraig nodded as Layla sighed.

"Shit," she said, quickly apologizing to Pop Pop for her language before he had a chance to say anything to her. "That's my fault. I was texting with Emmy on Thursday, asking how her date with Lucas's friend went. Joey was with me. When I told him who I was talking to, he said he thought Emmy was Paddy's girlfriend. I explained that you guys are just friends," she said to Padraig. Before he had a chance to correct her, Layla continued, "I didn't realize he wanted to ask her out. I mean, I love my brother dearly, but Joey is a player from the word go. I would have set her up with Gio or Luca."

"Not Tony?" Finn asked curiously.

Layla shook her head. "No, Tony's a bit too intense for her, I think. Oh well," Layla said as if it was no big deal.

"Who knows? Maybe Joey and Emmy will hit it off and get married. She would rock as a sister-in-law."

And then, oblivious to the bomb she'd just dropped on Padraig's head, Layla headed toward the large table she and Finn were sharing with their third, Miguel, and the other Moretti brothers.

Finn remained behind, studying Padraig's face closely. Not that he had to look too hard. Padraig wasn't bothering to hide his feelings at the moment.

"Emmy told the girls that she asked you out before Christmas and you turned her down. That you insisted on just being friends," Finn said, as if that would help.

Pop Pop shook his head. "Oh, Paddy."

"You've changed your mind, haven't you?" Finn asked.

Padraig nodded. "Yeah. I have."

Uncle Ewan walked over. "Hey. Is Emmy here with Joe Moretti?"

Padraig might have laughed at all the men in his family swarming around, ready to do battle with him, if he weren't so pissed off. And while he was angry at Joe, he was more furious with himself. He'd taken Emmy for granted for too long, unable to see what was standing right in front of him, too blinded by grief and guilt.

"I fucked this all up," he confessed.

"What the hell is going on over there?" Uncle Aaron asked, walking up to join them while pointing out Emmy and Joe in the booth together.

This time, Padraig couldn't hold back. He laughed and shook his head. "We're all discussing my stupidity. Join the party."

Emmy glanced over at the group of men staring at her—none of whom even attempted to play it cool by turning away. Though their faces were turned away from him, Padraig was fairly certain they were presenting a united front in scowling overprotectiveness.

She caught Padraig's eye and raised her eyebrow. "Told you so," she mouthed before turning her attention back to Joe, who was also aware that the two of them had captured attention. She leaned in, saying something that had him laughing loudly.

Pop Pop turned back around and stared him down. "So, my boy, how are you going to fix this?"

That was the ten-million-dollar question, wasn't it?

EMMY HAD TO ADMIT THAT AS FAR AS DATES WENT, THIS one with Joe was the best so far, if she didn't count the practice one with Padraig last weekend. Which she was trying to tell herself she couldn't count.

The Collins men had proven her right as they'd all converged around the bar, shooting evil glares at Joe, as if to warn him they were watching. When she'd told Joe that's what they were doing, he was amused and, scoundrel that he was, he'd upped his game, placing his arm around her shoulder, toying with her hair, whispering sexual innuendoes in her ear that had her laughing and blushing in equal measure.

She'd just ordered a third glass of wine, though she'd be smart to leave it untouched. She was feeling warm and fuzzy from the first two glasses and from Joe's attention.

Okay. That was a lie.

While she was having fun with Joe and was flattered by his flirting, it was Padraig's constant stare that had her all hot and bothered.

With the wine flowing through her veins, she gave up all pretense of accepting his *just friends* request. Instead of acknowledging that Padraig's continual glances were the act of an overprotective friend, she allowed herself to pretend he was actually jealous.

And while she knew she was being stupid, she didn't care. For one night, it felt good to let herself believe that Padraig could care about, could love her, the way he had Mia.

The stories he'd told her last Sunday about his late wife had done two things: made her admire Mia's incredible strength and courage, and ensured that she fell even more desperately in love with Padraig.

She glanced toward the stage when Hunter started playing one of her favorite songs. Tonight's entertainment was being provided by Hunter Maxwell, Aubrey Summers, Teagan Collins, and Sky Mitchell, all members—either by birth or through marriage—of the Collins family. They'd each come to fame through their music, and all of them—with the exception of Aubrey—were still touring regularly.

Aubrey was married to Padraig's cousin, Fergus, and was currently eight and a half months pregnant with her first child. As such, Fergus was never more than five feet away from her, clearly ready to whisk her away to the hospital at the first twinge of labor pain. Despite her huge belly, she'd pulled a stool onto the stage and sung half a dozen of her most famous songs.

Hunter had now taken over for the next hour or so and then, according to Sunnie—who'd stopped by the table she was sharing with Joe—Teagan and Sky planned to entertain them until closing.

If Hunter, Aubrey, Teagan, and Sky's names ever appeared on a marquee together, fans across the world would lose their collective minds and pay any amount of money for the concert tickets. Yet, here was Emmy, sitting in an Irish pub, listening to them perform like it was just any regular old

Friday night. It was times like these when she wished her mom—the world's biggest Teagan Collins fan—was still alive.

"Can I ask you something, Emmy?" Joe said after polishing off his second bottle of Peroni.

"Sure."

"Are you sure you and Padraig are just friends?"

She frowned. "Of course. Why?"

"Because the way he's been looking at you, watching us, is not the way a man looks at a woman who's just a friend."

Emmy glanced back toward the bar and saw...exactly what Joe did. She'd spent the last hour or so trying to convince herself it was her mind playing tricks on her.

But now...

Was Padraig jealous?

"I asked him out on Christmas Eve and he turned me down. But then, last Sunday..." She paused, debating whether or not this was the sort of thing she should talk about on a first date. Then she decided to heck with it. Maybe a man's perspective would help.

"Last Sunday?" Joe prompted.

"He came over to help me pick out an outfit for a date I was going on. Then he offered to help me practice my small talk."

"He must be a great teacher, because I wouldn't have thought you'd need any help with that. You're easy to talk to."

"So are you. I've had a lot of fun tonight," she said. "The thing is, Paddy also...well, he kissed me good night. Said it was practice too. But..."

"It didn't feel like practice."

Emmy shrugged. "Or maybe I just don't want to believe that's all it was."

"You've got it bad for the guy."

She nodded slowly. "But I know he doesn't feel the same way, so I'm moving on."

"Moving on, huh? Tell you what. I'm going to make you a promise right here and now."

"What kind of promise?" she asked.

"I promise to make you a very, *very* happy woman tonight."

Emmy liked the sound of that and she could now see why, according to his sister, Joe was so successful with women.

Emmy really liked him. She liked all the Morettis, actually. They were loud and brash and opinionated but, as her mother liked to say, "good people."

Unfortunately, she was doing the same thing to Joe as she had to Brian on Wednesday. Holding him up to the Padraig standard when what she really needed to do was get her head in the game.

Joe was charming, funny, sexy as sin and, if Layla was to be believed, a confirmed bachelor who wasn't looking for anything more than a good time. So maybe she'd been a fool for accepting a date with him. After all, she was dating with an eye toward a relationship that would hopefully—eventually —lead to marriage and a family.

Or...maybe it was time she stopped trying so hard to find a boyfriend—her mom always said the best way to find something was to stop looking too hard—and focused her energy on getting laid instead. She was long overdue, and Joe seemed like the perfect man for a hot one-night stand. Unlike her last one, Emmy was pretty damn sure she wouldn't regret spending the night with Joe for a single second.

Besides, it was past time for her to double down on her plan to move forward. No more Padraig comparisons. It wasn't fair to her dates. Yvonne said she'd need to kiss a lot of frogs to find her prince, and while Joe was a million miles away from a frog, she wasn't so green in the dating arena not to know he wasn't "the one."

But he could be her segue. Sex with a gorgeous, charismatic man to get her feet—and other parts—wet, and then she'd set up another date tomorrow with one of the guys from the dating app.

"Very happy, hmmm? And how do you propose to do that?" she asked.

Before Joe could respond, Yvonne, who was carrying a tray of empty drinks slipped on a wet spot on the floor near their booth. While she didn't fall, several of the glasses on the tray tipped over and half a glass of water splashed down Emmy's left side.

Yvonne gasped. "Oh my God, Emmy! I'm so sorry."

Emmy laughed, brushing off as much of the wetness as she could with her hand. "It's okay, Vonnie. It's only water."

"Let me get a towel."

Emmy waved her off. "No. I'm just going to pop into the restroom and grab some paper towels to dry off. Excuse me for just a moment, Joe."

"When you get back, what do you say we hit the dance floor?"

"I'd love that."

She stood and made her way across the room. As she did so, she felt Padraig's gaze following her. Before entering the restroom, she glanced back and saw him delivering their drinks to the table, then kneeling to wipe up Yvonne's spill.

He and Joe conversed amicably, and she sighed.

So much for the jealousy theory.

"Hey, thanks," Joe said as Padraig placed the drinks on their table.

"You two having a good time?" Padraig asked, fighting hard to be friendly as he bent down to wipe up the spilled water. He liked Joe. He really did. He just hated his guts at the moment.

"Yeah. Emmy's a sweetheart. Pretty as hell too. Can't believe a woman like her is still single."

Padraig nodded but didn't reply. Because it was on the tip of his tongue to tell Joe she wasn't single. But he figured he should drop that bomb on Emmy first.

In truth, he hadn't come over here to make small talk with Joe. His intention was distraction. "Hey, I wanted to let you know Aunt Riley has a buffet of appetizers set up on Sunday's Side. She just brought out a big platter of potato skins."

Joe's eyes lit up. "Oh yeah? I might head over and grab a plateful for me and Em. Thanks."

Padraig pasted on a fake smile, trying not to lose his cool over Joe calling her Em—who the fuck did this guy think he was?—and pretended to head back to the bar as Joe took off in the direction of the buffet table.

However, instead of returning to his station, Padraig detoured to the hallway that led to the restrooms. He didn't have long to wait before Emmy emerged.

"Hey, Paddy," she said when she saw him there. "Looks like everything is going great with the soft opening. Does this mean the pub is ready to open for business?"

He nodded, even less willing to make small talk with *her* than he'd been with Joe. "Yeah, it does. So about you and Joe Moretti—" he started.

She grinned. "Looks like third time's a charm. After the failed coffee and happy-hour dates, I'm relieved to say this one is a success so far."

"You know Joe lives in Philadelphia." He didn't have a clue why he spouted that nonsense. It wasn't what he'd intended to say at all. Of course, after watching her and Joe flirt all night, his ability to think and reason beyond that of a caveman was completely gone. At this point, he was surprised he hadn't fashioned himself a club out of one of Aunt Riley's baguettes and attempted to drag Emmy out of the pub by her hair.

"I know where he lives. So?" she prompted, no doubt confused by his ridiculous statement.

"Long-distance relationships are hard."

Her eyes widened with amusement. "Oh my God. It's just one date. Way too soon to start labeling it a relationship."

"Good."

She tilted her head. "Is it?"

"You need to be careful. The guy's a player, Em."

Emmy leaned closer. So close, he caught a whiff of the apple scent in her hair. His dick twitched. Jesus, he was definitely a goner if he got a hard-on from just smelling her shampoo.

Her lips were near his ear when she said quietly, "I don't have a problem with Joey's reputation because I'm hoping he'll want to play with *me*. It's been a long, painful dry spell, Paddy. My girlie bits are screaming at me."

She laughed, but the sound was cut short when he didn't join in. In fact, her forehead creased in confusion, and he could only assume he'd taken her off guard with his angry scowl.

"You're not *playing* with Joe Moretti," he said darkly.

"Excuse me?" she asked, a tinge of disbelief—and annoyance—in her voice. He'd never seen her annoyed before. Hell, he'd never seen Emmy lose her temper or become angry either. The woman was as peaceful and easygoing as a Sunday morning.

"Hey, there you are," Joe said, stepping next to Padraig.

"Bribed Hunter with a beer to play a slow song for us. Gives me an excuse to wrap my arms around you."

She narrowed her eyes playfully. "I don't know. Your sister has warned me about you. Not sure dancing is a safe activity for us."

Joe grinned wickedly. "I promise to be a perfect gentleman."

"You sure you want to make that promise? A perfect gentleman would behave appropriately, keeping his hands on my waist."

He seemed to consider that, then reached out to her. "Lots of gray area there," he joked.

She shook her head, giggling. "No, there's not."

"Appropriate means different things to different people, Em. As a writer, I think you'd understand the nuances of words." Joe, the asshole, backed his comment up with a wink that had Padraig clenching his fist.

"That is the biggest bunch of bullshit I've ever heard, Joey," she said.

"Thought I told you to call me Joe, gorgeous. As in, you're a god, Joe. And yes, Joe. More."

Emmy's laugh was husky, flat-out sexy. Padraig wasn't sure where this flirtatious woman had come from, but he sure as fuck didn't like it...directed at someone who wasn't him.

"Em," Padraig said, but Emmy's attention was firmly on Joe.

"How about, you're incorrigible, Joey?" she teased.

"Call me Joey one more time and I'll have to punish you."

"Promises, promises," she said in pure minx fashion, lightly slapping Joe's cheek.

Jesus. Christ.

Padraig wanted her. Bad.

"Come on. Let's dance," she said, placing her hand in Joe's

and letting him lead her away from Padraig and onto the dance floor.

Padraig cursed himself up one side and down the other for not saying what he'd pulled her aside to say. For not getting her the fuck away from Joe.

"Seriously, bro," Colm said, sidling up to him. "You gonna let Moretti steal your girl right out from under your nose?"

"Haven't exactly told her she's my girl yet, have I?"

"Having second thoughts?" Colm asked.

"Never been more sure of anything in my life."

Colm's wide smile proved he liked that answer. "Good. But I've gotta tell you, the rest of the family is starting to get antsy. You need to put them out of their misery. Pop Pop is fit to be tied. That Joe Moretti is a good-looking bastard. If you're making your move, make it fast. I told Dad I'd tend bar with him the rest of the night."

"You're shit at mixing drinks," Padraig said absentmindedly, unable to take his eyes off Emmy and Joe dancing. So far, the guy was keeping his hands on her waist, but even that touch was too much for Padraig's liking. Plus, they were dancing close. Way too close.

"Then I guess it's a good thing it's mainly family tonight. You and I both know all I'll be doing is draining the keg of Guinness. Any fool can pull a tap."

"Says the fool who pulled the tap so hard one night, he broke it off. All I asked you to do was cover the bar for ten minutes so I could go upstairs and change out of a shirt I'd stained with cranberry juice."

Colm chuckled, looking unremorseful. "One mistake, asshole. And I was three sheets to the wind. You're the clown who asked a drunk guy to man the bar." Colm nudged Padraig with his shoulder. "You've been different since we got back from Ireland. Happier, more like your old self. I'm glad. And before you say it, it doesn't have a damn thing to do with the fact we're standing back in this pub."

Padraig couldn't deny his brother's observation because it was true. The change in him had started with Pop Pop's pep talk in Ireland and grown stronger ever since returning to Baltimore and seeing Emmy again. "It doesn't. Or it's not *just* because of the pub. It's her. It's been her for a long time."

"So go get her."

❦ 6 ❦

Emmy laughed as Joe's hand slipped the tiniest bit lower on her back, skirting very close to touching her ass. Layla was right. He was a shameless flirt.

"I think our date is about to come to a close," Joe said out of the blue, just as the slow song was about to end.

She tilted her head, confused. The night was still young. "What do you mean? Do you need to leave?"

"Nope. But after this dance, I'm gonna go hang out with my family at their table."

"Joe," she said, wondering what the hell had gone wrong. She thought they'd been having a lot of fun. "Did I do something...say something..."

"Hell no. This has been one of the best dates I've had in a long time. It's just..."

"What?"

"You're not single, Emmy."

She studied Joe's face, trying to recall how much he'd had to drink tonight. He didn't act drunk. "I'm very single. Painfully, excruciatingly single."

"Yeah? You're wrong about that, and I'm gonna prove it."

"How?" she asked.

"I'm going to grab my good-night kiss now."

She didn't have time to react before he lowered his head and kissed her. It was a surprisingly gentle kiss. Soft. Too soft. It felt more friendly than passionate. She would have expected Joe's kisses to be more like...Padraig's. Joe seemed like the type of guy who would know his way around a kiss. Instead, this felt, well, lukewarm. Like he was phoning it in.

"I want to have a word with you, Moretti. *Now*."

Emmy jerked back, surprised by Padraig's deep—angry—voice so close to them on the dance floor.

"So I'm Moretti now, huh?" Joe asked, grinning, despite the outright fury on Padraig's face that seemed to scream danger.

"You and I need to talk," Padraig continued.

Emmy didn't often lose her temper, but Padraig was taking this overprotective routine to new levels, and it was pissing her off. What the hell was wrong with him?

"Padraig, listen—" she started.

"I think we should step outside," he added.

Neither man seemed to notice she'd spoken. Which infuriated her even more. They were facing off like two boxers in a ring, waiting for the bell to sound the beginning of the round.

Joe shook his head, heedlessly leaning closer to Padraig. Apparently a fool and his head *are* soon parted, because Padraig's fists were clenched and there was a fury in his eyes she'd never seen before.

"We don't have a damn thing to talk about, Padraig. But I think you have a lot of things you need to say to her." Joe jerked his head toward Emmy.

Emmy wasn't sure why that comment took the wind out

of Padraig's sails, but it certainly seemed to. His gaze softened as he looked at her. "Yeah. I do."

"You and I don't have a beef with each other," Joe continued. "I was just saying good night to my date. But heads-up, man. You leave her alone again, I'm gonna grab the chance you're not—and I won't back down a second time."

Padraig's expression seemed chiseled in stone, his jaw was clenched so tightly. "So noted."

"Good." Then Joe gave Emmy a quick kiss on the cheek, laughing deeply when Padraig growled. "Good night, Emmy. I had a great time." Then he actually had the audacity to wink at Padraig as he said, "You kids have fun tonight," before walking away.

That was it?

Her date was over?

Emmy turned to Padraig, hands on her hips, her temper spiking. "What the hell do you think—"

Before she could say more, Padraig grasped one of her hands and tugged her toward the back of the pub.

"Paddy," she said, digging her heels in. "Dammit. Stop!"

He spun to face her, and she gasped at the expression on his face, trying to figure out what the hell she was looking at. Best she could come up with was furious hunger.

Was that a thing?

"Walk with me, Em, or I swear to God, I'll throw you over my shoulder and carry you."

"Where are we going?" she asked stupidly, taking a big step back when he lowered his shoulder, ready to make good on his threat.

"Emmy..." he growled.

She threw her hands up in the air. "I'll walk."

Satisfied, he grabbed her hand once more.

Her feet began to move, even as the romance writer in her

immediately committed his words to memory. Throw her over his shoulder and carry her? That was definitely going in a book.

Of course, the second that thought crossed her mind, she was instantly sorry she hadn't tested him, just to see if he'd do as he threatened.

They reached the door to the storage closet, Padraig opening it and pushing her inside.

Once the door closed behind them, she whirled on him, ready to demand answers.

"You better explain to me what the fuck you—"

Emmy didn't get to finish that question either. Padraig kept steamrolling over her.

Not that she minded this time. Not when he gripped her shoulders and pulled her toward him, kissing her deeply.

Like last week's kiss, this one rendered her completely senseless as well. All capability of thinking or reasoning simply vanished as he plundered her mouth with his demanding tongue.

She wrapped her arms around his neck and held on. It was either that or melt into the floor, her body boneless under his delicious attack.

Padraig paid absolutely no heed to the appropriate waist zone, his hands running up and down her back, over her hips, then reaching lower to cup her ass. He used that grip to draw her even closer, his erection hard against her stomach.

Jesus.

His erection...

She tried to break the kiss, needing air, needing answers, but Padraig tightened his hold.

"Not yet," he murmured against her lips. He was gentling his kiss, but he wasn't letting her go.

"Paddy," she whispered.

He shook his head. "No," he insisted again. "Not yet. I'm not done."

She jerked slightly, then shivered when she felt him pull her blouse free of her jeans, slipping his hands underneath, his fingers stroking the bare skin at her waist. Her pussy clenched in response. Actually, everything clenched in response.

"God," she breathed, when his hands shifted north, engulfing her breasts. He pinched her nipples, more roughly than she would have expected, the pain setting off some sort of sensual current that had her rolling her hips against him.

Why were they wearing so many clothes? Because suddenly, all she could picture was him stripping her blouse and bra off, dragging her jeans down, and taking her against the shelves.

Oh my God. They were in the pub. His entire family was just outside this storage closet.

Had he locked the door?

Was there a lock on the door?

She pushed against him more firmly this time. If she didn't stop him now, she was going to spontaneously combust. "Paddy, please."

He relinquished her lips, his forehead pressed against hers.

"What are you doing?" she asked.

"Kissing you."

"Practice kissing?"

He scowled. "No!"

She blew out an exasperated breath. "Then what?"

"I didn't like seeing you with Joe Moretti."

Emmy frowned. "Is this an overprotective thing? Or..." She wouldn't let herself ask if he was jealous. Her self-preservation genes were finally kicking in. She'd been wearing her heart on her sleeve for too long and her pride was tired of taking a beating.

"No. Not overprotective," he said, placing one soft kiss on her lips. Then another. His sweet kisses were as deadly to her libido—and her heart—as his hungry ones.

"Then what?" she prompted, praying he'd say the word her heart longed to hear, the one that would mean he felt something for her stronger than friendship.

And then...she got her wish.

"I was jealous, Em. I've been seeing red ever since you walked in the pub with him. Spent the last couple of hours fighting the need to walk over and punch the guy's lights out."

She slowly shook her head. "But you said—"

"That kiss last week wasn't practice, and it wasn't me reaching out to you because I was sad about Mia. And I want you to forget everything I said on Christmas Eve because I was wrong. I was lying to myself *and* you. I can't just be friends with you anymore, Emmy."

Emmy was tempted to pinch herself, simply to make sure she was awake. Because she'd dreamed about him saying those words to her at least a million times. She was afraid to believe this wasn't some figment of her imagination.

"You can't?" she asked quietly.

"No. I can't. Go out with me. On a date."

She smiled. "Okay."

"Tomorrow night."

She nodded. "That works."

"I'll pick you up at six."

"I'll be ready."

"Get rid of that damn online dating app and cancel any plans you've made with other guys. I'm the *only* man you're dating from now on."

His tone was nothing short of demanding, and she felt like

maybe she should call him out for it. But the lonely woman who'd read way too many dark mafia romances lately was secretly thrilled by the possessiveness in his gaze. No one had ever looked at her like that.

"I don't have any other dates scheduled," she admitted.

"Good."

Ah, and now she understood what all those "goods" meant.

"Wear that black skirt and the indecent hot-pink shirt," he added with a wicked grin.

She laughed and started to shake her head. She really should put her foot down on him trying to control what she wore. However, her refusal never came.

Especially after he added, "And don't wear any panties."

Emmy's mouth fell open, a small squeak of shock emerging.

Something Padraig clearly found amusing, as he placed a finger under her chin, pushing her mouth closed, so he could resume their kiss.

A kiss that was interrupted when the door to the storage closet opened. She and Padraig broke apart as Ewan walked in and caught sight of them.

"Dammit. We're going to have to initiate some sort of signal," Ewan declared, unremorseful about barging in. "A napkin hanging on the doorknob or something. There's always somebody making out in this damn closet."

"There is?" Emmy asked.

"Caught Teagan and Sky in here the first night they met. I gotta say, I'm relieved to see you're both wearing your own clothes. That night, Sky ended up in Teagan's skirt."

"Do I want to know why?" Emmy asked, unable to resist, always a fan of his family's stories.

"Paparazzi. It was the only way to get him out of the pub

without being mobbed. I've also walked in on Tris and Lane a couple of times, Hunter and Ailis, Yvonne and Leo, Kelli and Colm..."

Emmy and Padraig laughed as he continued to rattle off names, including most of the family on his list.

"Sounds to me like you're the problem," Padraig said to his uncle. "Always coming in unannounced."

"Hey, don't blame me. I just work here. Not my fault if everyone has declared the closet Lover's Lane," he added, reaching for a large jar of pickles.

"What about you and Aunt Natalie? Find it hard to believe you two have never snuck in here," Padraig said.

Ewan shook his head. "Nope. Never made out with Nat in here. We're classier than that. Save our sexy workplace encounters for my office over on Sunday's Side. Got a nice big desk and office chair. Lots of possibilities. *Plus*, there's a lock on that door. I'm nobody's fool." Ewan chuckled as he left them alone once more.

Padraig wrapped his arm around her waist, intent on picking up where they'd left off, but Emmy placed her hand flat against his chest, holding him back.

"About that panties declaration," she said with a grin.

"Nonnegotiable." He backed up that statement with a quick, hard kiss that sent a flood of wanton thoughts through her head. "But test me if you want to," he said darkly. "Because I saw how you responded to Joe's threat to punish you—and I'm definitely down to carry through with that. Either way, you *will* be panty-less on our date."

"Have you been reading my books?" she whispered before she could think better of her question. It was just...it felt as if this Padraig had been ripped from the pages of one of her stories. Because she didn't just read about super alphas, she wrote them too.

As a friend, Padraig was affable and easygoing. But this man...

God, he was every fantasy she'd ever had, come to life.

He looked at her curiously. "I don't know your pen name, remember? Though I think you're going to have to give it to me now. I'm getting the impression I'd really like reading what you've written."

She leaned up, kissing him rather than responding. It was the first kiss she'd initiated, and Padraig let her control it, let her explore his lips at her leisure. She felt the heat from his breath, tasted the bitterness from the Guinness he'd been sipping, loved the way his hands stroked her back firmly, holding her as if he'd never let her go.

"Emmy," he murmured against her lips. "We better go back out to the pub, or this is going to go too far in a room with no lock. Besides, our first time is *not* going to be in a storage closet."

"Should we ask to use Ewan's office? Since it's classier and all."

Padraig laughed loudly, shaking his head. "Nope. Our first time is going to be in a bedroom. We'll christen the pub later."

She giggled, then tucked her blouse back into her jeans before accepting the hand he proffered.

They walked back out to the pub, and Emmy blushed slightly when she realized practically every member of the Collins family had noted their return *and* the fact Padraig was holding her hand.

Padraig's Pop Pop raised his Guinness to her in a silent toast, winking at her as he did so.

Emmy started for the bar, ready to claim her spot at the end, but Padraig tugged her in the opposite direction.

"Where are we going?"

"Colm said he'd work the bar for me tonight. Thought it might be nice if we actually got to sit together rather than separated by that counter."

He purposely led her to the booth she'd shared with Joe earlier, claiming the other man's place with a shit-eating grin.

Emmy glanced across the room and spotted Joe watching them. He was smiling widely, obviously pleased with himself, and that was when she realized all his flirting had been done simply to provoke a response from Padraig.

He'd followed through on his promise to make her a very happy woman.

"Thank you," she mouthed.

He gave her a thumbs-up, then turned his attention back to the conversation at his table.

Teagan and Sky took the stage, and the rest of the night felt like something out of a dream.

The two of them danced, ate, drank, and laughed with reckless abandon, as every member of the family found a moment to stop by their table to chat.

Sunnie and Kelli had cornered her in the bathroom at one point, and she'd told them that Padraig had asked her out on a date. The three of them squealed like teenage girls in high school, laughing at themselves for their ridiculous behavior afterwards.

She and Padraig remained at the pub until the wee hours, closing the place down with Tris and Colm. Then, Padraig walked her to her apartment, his arm wrapped around her waist, tucking her close to share his body heat since the night was brutally cold.

Once they arrived, she dug into her purse for her keys, her heart racing, as she internally debated if she should ask him in for coffee...or sex.

She wanted to. Desperately. But she wasn't sure if he would think she was rushing things.

"Invite me in," Padraig murmured as she put the key in the lock. His arm was wrapped around her waist, his lips brushing her ear as he spoke.

"Come in."

She opened the door and his grip tightened as he walked inside with her, the two of them connected. Then he pushed the door closed and flipped the lock.

"If you think I'm going too fast, tell me now and I'll leave, Em."

She laughed, the sound breathy and—dammit—nervous. Regardless, she shook her head. "I was afraid you would think I was rushing things. I..."

The rest of her words never materialized because she forgot how to speak. Padraig turned her to face away from him so he could pull her coat off and drop it to the floor. The entire time, his lips traced a sensual line of kisses along her neck.

Emmy's head fell to the side, her eyes drifting closed as she was swept away by the incredible pleasure his kisses provoked.

"God," she whispered. "Paddy."

"You're so beautiful, Emmy."

She shifted, turning in his arms. Her intention had been to kiss him, but the moment their gazes locked, they both froze, lost in each other's eyes. She couldn't stop looking at him, couldn't convince herself this was really happening.

Padraig ran his knuckles softly down her cheek. "So beautiful," he murmured. He kissed her once more, then again, and again. "Want to make out on the couch?"

"Oh my God, yeah. I do."

Everything was so easy with Padraig. It always had been. Right from the beginning.

The two of them walked into the living room, sitting together on the couch. She sat facing him, but he shook his head. "You're too far away."

Reaching for her, he pulled until she was straddling his lap, their faces a mere inch apart.

"That's better," he said, as he started kissing her once more.

They'd shared no less than a hundred kisses since he'd pulled her into the storage closet. It seemed as if neither of them could stop, now that they'd started. Less than a few hours in, and she was already addicted to Padraig's lips.

Because he kissed her like it mattered.

Like *she* mattered.

She'd spent all of her adult life writing about romance, immersing herself in feelings she'd experienced far too infrequently but constantly longed for. Then she considered all the kisses she'd described in her romance novels. How she'd imagined what they might feel like so that she could find a way to put them into words.

There were no words for the way Padraig's kisses made her feel. At least none that came even close to the surfeit of emotions swimming through her at the moment.

Consumed.

Caressed.

Cherished.

Devoured.

And horny.

Mainly horny.

She grinned to herself when that word—probably the least romantic of them all—took root and emerged as the winner.

Padraig pulled away and gave her a quizzical look. "Something funny?"

She shook her head, unwilling to confess where her thoughts had taken her. "No. It's just...my happiness keeps slipping out."

Padraig chuckled. "Mine too."

Rather than resume the kiss, Padraig's gaze drifted lower, his fingers slipping the first button on her blouse free, then the second, and the third.

She sucked in an unsteady breath, nerves and arousal battling for dominance at the moment. The sound drew Padraig's attention and, after that, his eyes remained on her face as his fingers drifted down the side of her throat and lower, caressing the top of her breasts.

She took another wobbly breath, and his eyes narrowed slightly.

"It's been a long time," she whispered.

He kept touching her softly, his fingers stroking. "How long?"

She silently cursed herself for saying anything at all. "Um..." She pretended to think about it even though she knew exactly how long.

Padraig wasn't fooled by her stalling techniques and he lifted his hand, taking away those lovely, sweet touches. "How long?" he repeated.

"Four years."

He stilled for a moment. "Four years?"

She nodded.

"Boyfriend?" he asked.

She shook her head. "Not really. Just a guy I was seeing off and on."

"And before that?"

"A one-night stand shortly after my mom died. Not one of

my finest moments. And before you ask, before that was high school. I had a boyfriend during my junior year. Brandon. He was super sweet, so kind. It was instalove for both of us. He was my first."

Padraig frowned. "Just three lovers?"

Emmy really didn't want to answer that question, though her silence seemed to do so for her.

Of course, so did the math.

"Em," he said, her name coming out as breath, not sound. She hated it. Hated thinking he thought her too innocent, too inexperienced.

"My mom got sick. ALS is...I couldn't leave her alone. I didn't *want* to leave her alone. Then, well...shit kept falling apart all around me. My dad's heart attack, Sam coming home, then going to jail. Then I hit *The New York Times* best seller list and walked into Pat's Pub and..."

"And we met."

She nodded, reaching hard for humor. "Fast-forward two years later, and here we are."

Padraig didn't laugh. He didn't even smile. "Did you stop dating because of me, Emmy?"

She *really* didn't want to answer that.

"You did," he said, saving her from having to come up with a response.

"Not intentionally. Honest. It just sort of turned out that way. And I don't want you to think it's been a hardship," she said. "Because I've actually had mad, passionate sex hundreds of times over the past few years. It's just been with..." She wiggled her eyebrows, letting him fill in the blanks.

This time, Padraig did chuckle. "Those fictional characters you're in love with. What were their names again? Jamie, Ian, and...?"

"Eric," she joked. "Plus, some really good toys."

"Okay then," he said, lifting her off his lap, then grasping her hand to pull her up, until the two of them were standing by the couch. "No making out."

"Wait. What?" Emmy was ready to put her foot down. Hard.

However, rather than reply, Padraig tightened his grip on her hand and led her down the hallway to her bedroom. Since they were headed in the right direction, she didn't make a fuss.

He kicked the door closed when it was apparent her cats were planning to join them.

"They won't like that," she murmured.

"Tough."

"No making out?" she asked.

"No. I want to make love to you, Emmy."

❧   7   ❧

"Oh," Emmy said on a sigh. "Okay. Yeah."

Padraig smiled briefly, then pulled her into his arms, resuming the kisses they'd shared all night. Now that he'd opened the door and let her in, he couldn't stop touching her, tasting her.

Her confession about her limited sexual history—and partners—hadn't shocked him as much as she might have thought. If there was anything he'd learned about Emmy over the last two years, it was that she wasn't the type of woman who viewed sex as merely a physical act. For her, sex and love went hand in hand.

He could see it in the way she hung voraciously on every word and action of his cousins and brother as they'd fallen in love with their soul mates. In the beginning, she'd pretended to type on her laptop while eavesdropping on his conversations, something he'd teased her about quite a bit.

When it became obvious she was listening in, he started asking if she agreed with the relationship advice he'd offered Leo—who was falling hard for Yvonne—and Finn—who was struggling to come to grips that he was in love with both Layla and Miguel.

Eventually, his family actually started turning to *her* for romance advice. It was Emmy who'd told Colm exactly where he'd gone wrong when trying to win Kelli's heart.

And if that wasn't enough to prove sex was synonymous with love for Emmy, it was driven home when she admitted to being in love with the fictional characters she fantasized about. She couldn't even masturbate without love figuring into the equation.

When he considered all that, he decided that was probably why she was such a successful romance writer.

After several minutes, he broke the kiss. "I want to see you," he murmured, reaching for the buttons of her blouse. He'd already undone the top three, revealing her pretty white lace bra.

Emmy was half a foot shorter than him, her body slender. Her breasts weren't large, but they weren't small either. In his mind, they were just right.

Once he finished unbuttoning her blouse, he slid it off her arms. He ran the back of his fingers over the tops of her breasts once more, enjoying the way she shivered, her eyes drifting shut under the impact of her arousal.

He ran his lips along her soft cheek, then nipped at her earlobe, provoking a breathy laugh.

Reaching around her, he unfastened her bra and pulled it off.

He expected her to be shy with him, but Emmy was made of sterner stuff. Rather than blush or try to hide herself, she simply stood before him, letting him look his fill.

Lowering his head, he took one of her tight nipples into his mouth, sucking on it as she arched her back and moaned. Then he repeated the action on the other.

Emmy's hands made their way to the back of his head, her fingers grasping his hair, tugging.

When he lifted his head again, she wasted no time moving them to the next part. She gripped the hem of his shirt and pulled it over his head. Like him, she paused, wanting to look as much as touch.

He sucked in a breath when she ran her finger over the tiny heart tattooed on the left side of his chest, Mia's name in the middle of it. Her gaze captured his.

"She's a part of me," he said, his voice low, wondering what she thought of the tattoo. Last Sunday, she'd said more than a few times that she admired Mia, that she wished she'd gotten the chance to meet her.

Padraig had been touched by that.

"The people we've loved and lost will always be a part of us, Paddy. Mia helped mold you into the man you are today. The one I adore. Just like my parents helped shape me. I don't think you and I would be here together if not for our lives with them."

He pressed his forehead to hers and let her words soak deep. She always knew exactly what to say. "Emmy," he whispered.

"I love the tattoo, love that you had Mia in your life. I'm sorry it was for such a short time."

He swallowed deeply, then hugged her because it was absolutely impossible not to in that moment. He needed her in his arms like he needed his next breath. The hug ended when he felt her fingers at the button of his jeans.

Padraig shifted away so that he could watch her. She unfastened his jeans and then he took over, shoving them and his boxers down, toeing off his shoes.

Her gaze remained on his erection, and an adorable grin filled her face.

"That looks like way more fun than my vibrator," she joked.

Padraig laughed. "You ain't seen nothing yet."

Then he reached over, helping her out of her own jeans and panties. "Sit on the side of the bed."

Emmy did as he asked, then started to move back to make room for him.

He shook his head. "No. Stay right there."

Emmy gasped when he knelt on the floor in front of her, parting her thighs and tugging until her ass was at the edge of the mattress.

He wasted no time lowering his mouth to her opening, running his tongue along her slit. She was already wet. Soaking wet.

Padraig used the tip of his tongue to tease her clit, his hands resting on her upper thighs to hold her still. Drawing his tongue lower, he pushed it inside her pussy. She was hot and oh-so ready for him.

Emmy's hands flew to his head. "Holy shit. So much better than my toys."

He fucked her with his tongue before returning to her clit. Pressing two fingers inside her, he groaned at the tightness. Thrusting his fingers, he kept pressure on her clit with his tongue.

"Oh God," she cried. "That feels so good. Right there. Oh my God, right there," she said with a gasp when he curled his fingers inside her. "Please do that again!"

Padraig would obviously never have to guess what Emmy liked. She was a vocal lover and it turned him on.

He continued to stretch her with his fingers while teasing her clit with his tongue and teeth. He was determined her first orgasm would come from his mouth.

Padraig didn't have long to wait. Emmy fell over the edge

after only a few minutes, her body trembling as the pleasure of her orgasm washed through her. He continued to stroke her throughout, gritting his teeth over the impossibly tight clenching of her pussy.

It had been so long since he'd found his own pleasure with anything other than his hand. He'd actually resigned himself to the fact that jerking off was it for him, certain for so long that he'd never want to sleep with another woman.

Then Emmy walked into his life. And his heart.

And he realized there was something else they had in common. Because like her, nowadays, he needed love with his sex too.

Love.

Padraig lifted his head, then rose on unsteady legs, looking down at Emmy.

Her hands were thrown over her head, her eyes closed, her body flushed.

She was beautiful.

And his.

He loved her.

The realization hit him like a wrecking ball.

Her eyelids lifted and her gaze focused on him. That was when he realized he hadn't moved, hadn't spoken.

He couldn't begin to guess what she read on his face.

"Paddy," she whispered, lifting her arms toward him. "Please."

He closed his eyes, recalling a time when Mia had said those exact same words to him. They'd gone to the beach because she'd never seen the ocean. That night, in their hotel room, they'd made love. Mia had spoken his name with that one word. *Please.*

Then, like now, he'd been overwhelmed by the feeling of

love, his heart so full of the emotion he thought it would burst.

He didn't think Mia should be here—in his thoughts. Not when he was with Emmy. But he didn't know how to keep her out.

Padraig jerked when Emmy's hand slipped into his. He opened his eyes and noticed she'd sat up, her eyes studying his face. Seeing far too much.

"You haven't slept with anyone since her."

It wasn't a question. It didn't have to be. Emmy knew that truth.

"It's just..." He paused, unable to confess his feelings. He didn't want to hurt Emmy, didn't want her to think he wasn't one hundred percent here with her, in this moment. Because he was.

She smiled softly. "She keeps popping into your head."

He nodded.

Emmy patted the spot next to her on the mattress, and he sank down next to her.

"Do you still want to sleep with me?" she asked.

He didn't hesitate to respond. "More than anything."

The ends of her lips lifted slightly, the shadow of a grin that faded too fast. "Do you think you'd regret it if we did?"

"Never in a million years."

This time the grin lasted a second or two longer.

"Are you wishing that I was her?"

Emmy had the courage of a lion, asking one painful question after another, risking the hurt his answers could bring. Regardless of that, she didn't hold back.

"Jesus. No, I don't. Not at all, Emmy. Fuck. It's more like...disbelief."

"Disbelief?"

"I'm struggling to believe I can have this twice. I keep seeing Mia's face, and then I look at you and..."

"And?" she prompted, waiting for him to explain, but he wasn't sure he could. Or at least, he wasn't sure he could explain it well enough.

"I never thought I could feel this way again. That I could be with a woman who wasn't Mia and want her so damn much, it actually hurt. And I don't just mean physically. I want you, Emmy, utterly and completely...in every possible way. Body, soul, heart."

This time, she didn't merely grin. She smiled, her whole face filled with absolute joy. "That is *so* going in a book."

He chuckled, the sound cut short when she twisted, straddling his thighs, her arms wrapped around his shoulders, their position the same as the one on the couch. His rock-hard cock pressed between their bodies.

"You don't have to shut Mia out, Paddy. I don't want to erase your memories of her or rewrite your past. And I think it's only natural that you would think of her tonight. I'd be surprised if you didn't."

He kissed her, her words soaking into his skin like aloe on a burn. The kiss started slow, gentle, but it soon grew in strength, in passion, as he pressed her lips open with his, their tongues meeting, stroking.

Padraig turned them together, reclaiming her lips, refusing to release her for even a second. He pushed her to her back, following her down. His chest was flat against her breasts, his knees resting on the mattress between her outstretched thighs. She lifted her legs, wrapping them around his hips.

He shifted slightly, reaching between them to place the head of his cock at her opening and lifting his head, wanting to see her eyes as he pushed in.

Their gazes locked as he slowly slid inside, his body tight

with the need to go slow.

That attempt was made difficult by Emmy, who kept shifting, lifting, drawing him deeper.

Once he was seated to the hilt, he kissed her.

Then froze.

"Shit. Emmy," he whispered.

Emmy, as always, read his mind.

"I'm on birth control. It's fine."

He swallowed heavily, nodded, and set himself free. Padraig started thrusting slowly, but soon his movements grew faster, harder, hungrier.

Emmy was with him every step of the way, her fingers digging into his shoulders, her hips rising to meet him.

He grasped her legs beneath her knees, lifting her higher.

The change in position drove her to the peak in an instant. Emmy's eyes closed as she cried out. He gritted his teeth as she came, fighting with everything he had to hold back his own climax. He wasn't finished with her. Not by a long shot.

God. He'd never be done with her.

He slowed his motions but didn't stop fucking her through her orgasm. She shivered, her body loose, her limbs exhausted.

"Paddy," she said, her voice hoarse from her cries.

"One more, Em. I want you to give me one more." As he spoke, he pulled out, flipping her to her stomach. She flopped down on the mattress like every bone in her body had turned to liquid.

He chuckled, then slapped her ass. Just one hard, stinging smack.

Her reaction was exactly as he hoped. She gasped with shock, then wiggled her ass. "Do that again."

Padraig would have laughed if he could have spared the

breath.

He lifted his hand and brought it down on her other ass cheek. He alternated two more times, watching as Emmy came to life beneath him once more. She pushed up onto her knees but kept her head against the mattress.

"I want more," she said.

"Of the spanking? Or...?" He placed his cock back at her opening.

"That. I want that. God, please, Paddy. Take me. Hard."

He didn't need to be asked twice. Hell, he didn't need to be asked the first time. He thrust in roughly, quickly, giving her no time to adjust as he gave her exactly what she wanted.

The temperature in the room grew hotter, more humid, their bodies slick with sweat as they pounded into each other as if their lives depended on it.

Reaching around her, he found her clit, stroking it, determined she was going to come with him. She got there a split second before him, coming again—for the third time—and this orgasm was stronger than all the rest. Her keening cry mingled with his groans and curses as he came so hard, it was almost painful.

"Jesus, Em! Goddammit, sweetheart. *Fuck*."

Neither of them spoke as they fell down onto the mattress, the only sound in the room their labored breathing.

Padraig's heart was racing so fast, he thought he might have a heart attack.

Emmy lay facedown, her head turned away from him, so all he could see was her mass of long blonde hair.

"Turn around, Emmy," he said, needing to see her face, wanting to make sure she was okay, that he hadn't been too rough.

She twisted, revealing her flushed cheeks, her bright—if tired—blue eyes, and her cat-who-ate-the-canary grin, which told him all he needed to know. Emmy scooched over until her head rested on his shoulder, her arm around his waist. He tucked her even closer as he wrapped his arm around her and placed a kiss on top of her head.

"Okay?" he asked.

"So okay." She lifted her head and they kissed again, this one just a soft touching of lips. Crazy how it impacted him just as strongly as the longer, deeper, more passionate ones.

They lay together for several minutes, neither of them speaking. Their friendship had evolved incrementally over the past two years, until they'd reached a place where there was no such thing as awkward silence.

"You want to take a shower together before we turn in for the night?" he asked, realizing if he lay there too much longer, he'd fall asleep.

"You're staying?" she asked.

He hadn't considered that wasn't an option. "Of course. Unless you want me to leave."

She shook her head. "Oh no. I don't want you to leave. Not at all. I was only thinking about Seamus."

He loved that she was such an animal lover. It was something they had in common. "Half an hour before I broke up your date with Joe, I slipped out for a few minutes and took a walk to cool off. Went to my apartment and grabbed Seamus and his leash. We blew off some steam together. He'll be okay until morning."

"So the way you came out onto that dance floor, guns blazing, was *after* you blew off steam?"

"Hell yeah. If hadn't done that, I would have walked over to Joe and started the conversation without words, just fists flying. I have to admit...I've never been the jealous type. But tonight, I was eaten alive with it."

"I thought it was hot," Emmy confessed.

"Oh yeah?"

She nodded. "Never had a guy fight for me."

"I'm always going to fight for you, Emmy." The moment he said the words, he knew they were true.

"I'm always going to fight for you too," she said, her eyes brimming with happy tears. "Do you have to go into work tomorrow?"

"Nope. I'm off the rest of the weekend. Meeting with my dad, Ewan, and Keira Monday morning to discuss how the soft opening went. Figure we'll take a day or two to fix what needs fixing and then...we'll open. Besides, you and I have a date planned tomorrow night, remember?"

"I do. But we could just hang out here if you wanted."

"Nope. Taking my girl out for a fancy dinner."

"I like the sound of that."

"A fancy dinner?"

She shook her head. "Being your girl."

He liked the sound of that too.

"Well, if you won't let me cook you dinner, I'll make you breakfast in the morning then. I make a killer spinach and mushroom omelet."

"You like to cook?"

"I love it, but I don't do it much. Always seems like too much trouble, trying to cook for one."

"Yeah. I get that—eating alone sucks."

"It really does."

"Doesn't help that I'm not much in the kitchen. If I'm not eating at the pub, my dinners are usually cereal, soup, frozen pizza, or the yellow meal."

She gave him a curious look. "Do I want to know what the yellow meal is?"

Padraig laughed. "Mia dubbed it that. As she got sicker, I took over more of the meal prep. Like I said, I'm not a great cook. One of our weekly standards was the yellow meal. I threw a couple prepackaged chicken cordon bleu and some tater tots on a cookie sheet in the oven and then opened a can of corn so we could say we'd eaten a vegetable. Of course, I always added a dollop of ketchup for color because I'm a professional that way."

She laughed. "Do you promise not to judge me if I say that actually sounds pretty good?"

"I'll make it for you one night."

They both laughed when they heard a scratching at the door. "My cats sleep with me," she admitted.

"That might be a problem." She frowned briefly before he explained, "Because Seamus sleeps with *me*. You think Luna and Neville would be okay sharing a bed with my mutt?"

"Might make for some interesting nights," she said, before the weight of his words sank in. "You're planning for us to share a bed?"

"Every single night."

"Oh. Okay. Yeah."

He laughed at her surprised but obviously pleased response—the same one she gave earlier when he'd said he was going to make love to her. She stood up to cross the room and the second she opened the door, both cats streaked inside, jumping onto the bed. Neville—a huge Maine Coon—settled down at his feet almost instantly. Luna—the tiny Calico—prowled around him a couple of times before flopping down near his head.

Emmy returned to the bed, but she didn't get in. "You know," she said. "I've never showered with anyone before."

All traces of tiredness he'd felt vanished in an instant as Padraig rose from the bed. "I'll scrub your back if you scrub mine."

She giggled. "Deal."

❧ 8 ❧

Padraig pulled out Emmy's chair for her, and she smiled. "Thanks."

Her gaze traveled around the restaurant, taking in the white tablecloths, the candlelight, the soft piano music, the dim lighting.

Padraig ordered a bottle of Chardonnay from the waiter, who came to greet them as soon as they were seated.

The restaurant wasn't overly crowded, the tables spaced out enough that she could almost believe they were the only people in the place.

"How did you find this place? It's very romantic."

Padraig grinned. "Ryder told me about it. No shock there, right?"

They shared a laugh. Ryder was now married to Padraig's cousin, Darcy, but the couple had had a rocky start to their relationship due to Ryder's assertion that he didn't possess the love/romance gene. He'd been in an unhappy marriage prior to dating Darcy, and it had convinced him he wasn't "good husband material."

Darcy had taught him how wrong he was, and now he was the king of romance, always wooing his wife with flowers and candy and impromptu weekend escapes. Lately, most of the Collins males had begun complaining to Ryder about how he was making them look bad with their own wives.

"Of course he did," Emmy joked. "Well, be sure to thank him for the recommendation. This place is lovely." She looked around again, cataloging what she was seeing, certain this would be the perfect setting for a chapter in the book she was currently writing.

"You're mapping the place out, aren't you?"

She looked back at Padraig and giggled. "Guilty."

Padraig had been around her long enough that he understood her writer eccentricities, the way she would snap random pictures of places with her phone so that it would help her word her descriptions.

"So you're putting this place in a future book?"

"Actually, it will work great in my current story."

"Oh yeah? What's the book you're writing about?"

Emmy flushed. "Um...you know, the usual."

"You've never let me read one, so you'll have to spell out the *usual* part for me."

Emmy blew out a long breath. It was time to just rip off the Band-Aid and tell Padraig her pen name. The silly game had gone on long enough. The problem was...the more time she'd spent with his family, the steamier her stories had gotten.

Like off-the-charts hot.

"This is your family's fault," she murmured.

"My family?" he asked, confused by her comment. "What do they have to do with your books?"

"The last two years? Everything. I haven't exactly lied when I've mentioned certain things were going in my books.

Your family has the greatest love stories. I haven't struggled for a plot since the day I first walked into Pat's Pub."

Padraig chuckled, clearly amused to know that. "So you're not hiding your pen name as a joke. You're doing it because you've been stealing all of their stories."

"Stealing is a strong word," she said with a wink. "I've just been borrowing bits and pieces. I mean, the stories are definitely fiction, but I've borrowed some romantic lines, some dark moments, some of their meet-cutes."

"Dark moments and meet-cutes? I have no idea what you're talking about."

"Take Sunnie and Landon, for example. The way they'd been friends forever but found each other after that viral "hot cop saves sexy nurse" video. That was a brilliant storyline. So I took that concept and wrote a romance with that as the meet-cute. Basically, it's a fun and clever way to introduce the hero and heroine to each other."

"Gotcha. And the dark moments? I'm assuming that's a breakup or something?"

"It doesn't have to be a breakup, necessarily. Sometimes it's as simple as a misunderstanding—sort of like Colm completely screwing up his proposal to Kelli by listing a bunch of logical reasons why they should be together while totally forgetting to tell her that he loved her."

Padraig chuckled. "He really did fuck that up."

"And sometimes the dark moment is because of outside influences. Like how Fergus almost lost Aubrey to that crazy stalker."

"Dark moments. I get it. So have you written a stalker story?"

Emmy nodded. "That was the latest book to hit *The New York Times* best seller list."

"You realize my family would love to read these books. They sound awesome," he said.

"Well, the problem isn't the plot lines. It's the other things they've inspired me to write."

Padraig's brow furrowed in confusion. "Other things?"

Emmy felt the heat creeping up her neck, and she didn't need a mirror to know she was blushing.

Padraig's face cleared as he put two and two together. "And now we're getting to the good part. Tell me exactly who's been inspiring the other stuff."

Emmy rolled her eyes but answered him anyway. "Sunnie, Darcy, Yvonne...even Bubbles."

Padraig snorted. "Jesus. Not sure I want to know what you've learned from Bubbles."

"What? Are you serious? She's one of the most fascinating people I've ever met. She's influenced quite a few secondary sidekick characters in my books."

"You're killing me, Em. You gotta let me read one of these books."

She shook her head. "Nope. Too embarrassing."

He studied her face. "Embarrassing or enlightening?"

Padraig knew her way too well. Because she *had* written out a lifetime of sexual fantasies in her stories. "Touché."

"All the more reason you should let me read one, wouldn't you say?"

She lifted one shoulder, unwilling to answer that question. Not that it helped. Padraig wasn't ready to change the subject.

"Who gave you the idea for your current story?"

Emmy hesitated for a moment, then said, "Caitlyn."

Padraig's brows rose. "Caitlyn? Em...are you writing about BDSM?"

"You know about her relationship with Lucas?"

Padraig nodded. "Lucas and I have talked a bit. I wasn't aware *you* knew."

"I mentioned doing some research for this book to Sunnie. She suggested I talk to Caitlyn or Keira. I was too embarrassed to bring it up to your aunt, so I contacted Caitlyn. We met at her place while Lucas was at work. We split a bottle of wine and had a fascinating conversation."

"I'm sure you did."

"Why were you and Lucas talking about it?" she asked.

"Let's just say we have some similar...kinks."

Emmy's eyes widened. "You do?"

"We do. Tell me, Emmy. Do you have an interest in BDSM?"

Emmy took a sip of her wine, considering her answer. "Some parts of it, I suppose."

"Like?"

She grinned. "If I confess my sexual fantasies to you, I'm going to expect you to reciprocate."

"I think I already started. But this seems like a fun game. Why don't we go back and forth, fantasy for fantasy."

She put her wineglass down. "Fine. I'd like to be tied up in bed."

A sexy smile emerged on Padraig's face. "That's good. Because I'd love to tie you up."

"You would?"

He nodded.

"Have you ever..." She waved her hand around, letting him fill in the blanks.

Padraig chuckled. "For a sexy romance writer, you never seem to be able to say the words."

"It's easier to type them."

"Yes, Em. I've tied up a couple former lovers in my

younger, wilder days. So...bondage is now on the table. Good to know. What else should we add to our list?"

"This is a list? I thought it was a game and we were just chatting about sexual fantasies."

"It's a list," Padraig insisted. "So keep going."

"Fine. The heroes in my books are typically alpha males, guys who take charge in the bedroom."

Padraig toyed with the stem of his wineglass. "I don't have a problem with that."

"Obviously. Considering the fact I'm sitting here without any panties on."

Padraig reached under the table and touched her knee. His hand didn't drift any higher. Probably because he'd already confirmed her panty-less state back at her apartment.

The moment she'd opened the door, he'd pushed her inside, closed the door, and pressed her against it, kissing her as if he hadn't seen her in months rather than the few hours they'd separated this afternoon to prepare for their date.

He'd kissed her so senseless, she hadn't realized his hand had drifted under her skirt until his fingers grazed her bare ass. She'd gasped, then moaned when he'd run his fingertips along her embarrassingly wet slit, pleased to discover she'd done exactly as he'd asked.

Padraig removed his hand when the waiter returned to take their orders, and she was sorry when he didn't return it after the man left.

"Your turn," she whispered.

Padraig leaned closer. "I plan to expand on that spanking we toyed with last night, only next time, I'm taking you over my knee. I also want to initiate every room in both of our apartments. I'll bend you over the kitchen counters, the couches, the dining room tables, and take you from behind. You're going to give me blowjobs in both of our showers, and

I'm going to go down on you on the living room floors. I want to use every single one of your sex toys on you. We're going to experiment with anal—and I want you to give me your damn pen name because I intend for us to role-play every fictional couple you've ever created."

Emmy sat still, stunned into silence as she let herself imagine Padraig doing each and every thing he described.

When she failed to speak after several moments, Padraig laughed quietly. "Have I scared you off?"

She quickly shook her head. "Not at all."

"And now that I've confessed all that, I'm wondering if I can convince you that we should ask the waiter to pack up the food we just ordered as takeout so we can go back to my place and get started on that list tonight. I think we could put one hell of a dent in it."

"Tonight?" Not that Emmy wasn't willing to give it the college try, but damn...it was a heck of a list.

He reached across the table and took her hand. "I find myself very impatient when it comes to what I want to do with—and to—you."

"Can we take turns feeding each other?" she asked.

"Actually, I have something else in mind." Padraig raised his hand to call the waiter over, requesting their meals be boxed up and reassuring the man that nothing was wrong. He lied, claiming there was a small emergency at home. Fifteen minutes later, they were in Padraig's car and headed to his place.

"This is insane," Emmy said with a laugh. "How did this date get so out of control?"

Padraig winked at her. "You drive me wild, Em, and I like it."

They parked outside Padraig's apartment, and he held her hand as they climbed the stairs to his place. He handed her the bag of food. "Why don't you dip that out onto plates while I take Seamus out real quick? I have no intention of leaving this apartment for the rest of the night once we get started."

Emmy took the bag with a grin. "I like the sound of that."

Padraig grabbed Seamus's leash and they headed out together. Emmy started for the kitchen but detoured briefly when her gaze landed upon a wall of pictures in the living room. She'd been to Padraig's apartment loads of times and she'd seen all of his framed photos before.

He hadn't changed any of the pictures since she'd known him, even though she'd given him several new ones as gifts. Just this Christmas, she'd given him a framed photo she'd snapped of him with his Pop Pop at the pub a few weeks before the fire. Glancing around, she didn't see it—or the one of Seamus she'd given Padraig on his birthday, or any of the others for that matter—and she briefly wondered what he'd done with them.

Then she studied the pictures that were still there, unsure why she felt compelled to look at them again. Perhaps because she was perusing the pictures through different eyes as she now knew the stories behind them. Every photograph on the wall included Mia.

Emmy smiled sadly when she saw the selfie of Padraig and Mia standing before the Hogwarts Castle at Universal because she now knew about the horrible migraine that had ravaged Mia later that same night. Her heart panged when she saw the panoramic of Paris, and she recalled Padraig's wish that he'd been able to freeze time right there in that moment. She hoped there might come a time when he'd wish the same thing for them. And then there was the one of Padraig and Mia on their wedding day.

Emmy forced herself away from the photos, walking into

the kitchen. She grabbed some plates, dipping out their food. It smelled delicious. She left them on the counter and returned to the living room, allowing her hopes for the night to play out in her mind.

Emmy let the romance writer inside her take over as she closed her eyes, setting the scene. Reaching for a blanket that hung on the back of the couch, she spread it out over the floor, then tossed a couple of throw pillows on top. She turned off the overhead light, opting to illuminate the room with just one lamp.

Returning to the kitchen, she was touched to find a bottle of her favorite Chardonnay in his refrigerator. She uncorked it and poured a glass before popping the top on a bottle of Guinness for Padraig.

She heard Seamus and Padraig return, then she listened as he led the dog down the hall to his bedroom before meeting her in the kitchen.

"Thought we might enjoy our meal more if we didn't have that mutt of mine sitting next to us on the floor, begging."

She giggled. "I thought you were working on training him."

"I think you and I both know I'm shit when it comes to disciplining that dog. He's got me wrapped around his paw."

She and Padraig had had countless conversations about his untrained dog. Emmy had forwarded him information about a dog training course he could sign up for, but Padraig hadn't bothered. He'd confessed last week that his hesitance was based on the fact Seamus had actually been part of Mia's bucket list, her desire to own a "badly behaved" dog. It was the first time she'd understood his reluctance, even though she hadn't realized how deep Padraig's desire ran to keep things just as they'd been with Mia.

Her thoughts drifted to the photos again, to the fact he'd

never changed them.

Padraig reached for their drinks, while she grabbed the utensils and plates. It wasn't until he lifted his hands that she realized he was holding something else.

"What is that for?" she asked about the necktie as they walked to the living room together.

"You'll see." They set their plates on the coffee table, then dropped down to sit on the blanket she'd spread out.

Emmy started to reach for her meal and a fork, but Padraig shook his head. "Not yet."

Her heart rate increased when he began to unbutton her blouse. "Naked dinner?" she asked, her voice suddenly breathless.

"One of us is going to be naked."

"What about you?" Emmy's gaze narrowed.

"We'll get to me later."

She shook her head, but Padraig ignored her, continuing to strip off her clothing, her blouse and bra tossed to the side of the blanket before he urged her to her knees so he could unzip her skirt and tug it down her hips.

"Slip off your shoes," he said.

Emmy did as he requested, then reached out, intent on removing his clothes as well. He caught her wrists before she could touch him.

"Bad girl," he murmured, his tone suddenly deliciously dark and sexy.

"Paddy," she whispered, hearing the slight whine in her voice.

"You're mine, Emmy. Tonight, you're all mine."

She licked her lips, turned on by the possessiveness in his gaze. She leaned forward, needing more from him. With her hands still captive in his, all she could do was attempt to steal a kiss.

Padraig tugged her away from him when he shifted her hands from her front to her back. She struggled briefly when she felt him loop the necktie around her wrists.

"What—"

"Bondage, remember?"

When she'd played that fantasy out, she'd always seen herself in bed, her wrists bound to the headboard.

"But I—"

"Shh." Padraig knotted the tie and released her.

Emmy couldn't resist trying to tug her hands free. She realized he hadn't lied about his experience with bondage. The knot held.

With her arms secured behind her back, her breasts were thrust out, something Padraig took advantage of. He lowered his head, sucking one of her nipples into his mouth.

Her head fell back, her entire body tingling when he reached out and pinched the other nipple. "God, Paddy," she breathed.

He lifted his head, smiling widely, as he picked up her plate. "You said something about feeding each other?"

She twisted slightly to show him her bound hands. "I think that's going to be a little difficult for me at the moment."

Padraig shook his head. "Doesn't matter. We're doing this my way." He lifted one of the shrimp she'd ordered, from her plate, running it along her lower lip, her mouth watering over the scent of butter and Old Bay.

"Open up," he prompted.

She did so, allowing him to pop the shrimp into her mouth. She chewed slowly, then swallowed as he watched. Then he lowered his head and licked the trace of butter left behind on her lips.

"Delicious," he murmured.

Padraig picked up one of the fingerling potatoes next, offering her half, before taking the second half himself. The next time he offered her a shrimp, she took it and one of his fingers inside her mouth, sucking the butter from it seductively, loving the way Padraig's eyes darkened with desire.

He continued to feed her—and himself—from both of their plates until Emmy insisted she was too full for another bite. Between the two of them, they'd polished off her shrimp, his crab cake, half the potatoes, and most of the asparagus. Twice, he'd drawn the tip of the asparagus, drizzled with a cream sauce, around her nipple before sucking it off. It was hands-down the most erotic meal she'd ever consumed. Padraig kissed her throughout, the two of them sharing everything they tasted.

The entire meal had been eaten from his fingers, with her naked and him fully dressed, which Emmy found ridiculously sexy.

"Don't move," Padraig said, rising with the plates. He took them to the kitchen and she listened as he washed his hands. When he returned, he didn't rejoin her on the blanket. Instead, he stood before her.

Emmy's gaze drifted to the bulge beneath his dress pants, and she licked her lips.

"You're so fucking sexy, Emmy."

He was the only man to ever make her feel that way. Padraig made her want to do wild, wicked, wanton things. He gave her the confidence to actually try the things she'd only ever been daring enough to write down.

She pushed herself up onto her knees, her legs splayed, her submissive pose not lost on either of them.

Padraig unfastened his pants, slowly pulling down the zipper. She wasn't the only one who'd gone out to dinner commando. He winked at her when she realized he'd bypassed the boxer briefs.

Once his pants were open, he reached in and drew out his erect cock. "Look at me," he demanded. "Let me see your eyes when you take me into your mouth."

Emmy followed his command, resisting the urge to close her legs in search of some sort of stimulation. If her hands were free, she'd touch herself. She was too turned on, too needy.

Padraig guided the head of his cock to her lips and she parted them, her tongue darting out, teasing, tasting. His hands drifted to her hair, his fists closing around it as he pressed in deeper.

"I'm never going to get enough of you."

She felt the same way.

Padraig used his grip on her hair to set the pace, the depth. Emmy clenched her bound hands together, her eyes never leaving his.

She could sense he was getting close, his breathing more halting. Just before he came, he withdrew.

"No," she said, but Padraig was already leaning over, his hands beneath her arms, lifting her. Her world went topsy-turvy when he spun her around, bending her over the arm of his couch.

He wasted no time, driving inside her. The gentle lover from the night before had vanished, all traces gone, as Padraig took her like a man possessed.

Reaching around her waist, he found her clit, stroking it until she saw stars. Emmy closed her eyes tightly, her toes clenching as an orgasm crashed over her with the force of an avalanche.

"Holy shit," she cried out.

Padraig was just two strokes behind her, his hands gripping her hips tightly, holding her in place as he came inside her.

"Emmy. Jesus, Emmy."

She sank down, her cheek pressed against the couch cushion, Padraig's body folded over hers, his chest against her bare back.

She belatedly realized he was still essentially dressed, his shirt in place, his pants open but on.

They remained that way for a few minutes, both of them struggling to catch their breath. Then she felt the tie on her wrists give way. Padraig helped her stand, his hands on her shoulders, massaging them before turning her and pulling her into his embrace.

He kissed the top of her head. "Just so you know, that was only the beginning. We're knocking a few more things off that list tonight because I'm not finished with you. Not by a long shot."

She stretched up on tiptoe to kiss his cheek. "Good," she said softly. Then she moved until her lips touched his ear, and she whispered something so softly, she wasn't sure he heard, especially when he frowned, confused.

Then the light went on, and Padraig smiled widely, his gaze finding hers. "Is that...?"

"My pen name," she murmured. "And since we're knocking things off our list, I feel like I should tell you, I regret walking to the storeroom closet willingly after you threatened to throw me over your shoulder."

Padraig laughed. "You regret that, huh?"

She nodded.

"Game on," he replied, picking her up, throwing her over his shoulder firefighter style, and carrying her to his bedroom as she laughed delightedly.

Game on indeed.

❈   9   ❈

adraig hummed as he wiped up the counter, his thoughts drifting back to kissing Emmy goodbye before he left for work. They'd spent the entire morning and afternoon lounging in each other's arms, watching TV, eating breakfast and lunch in bed, and making love countless times.

It had been two weeks since their first date, and Padraig couldn't recall the last time he'd been this happy. It had been years.

"Jesus, man. You gotta wipe that grin off your face. People are going to start to think you're touched in the head."

Padraig looked up and laughed at Finn's observation as his cousin grabbed a stool at the bar, a big plate of wings in his hands. Then his brows rose when he spotted Oliver and Lochlan just a few steps behind, carrying clean plates, napkins, and wipes.

"Did I miss an invite to the party?" Padraig asked, pulling down three pint glasses and filling them with Guinness from the tap. He'd never had to take an order from these guys. Like him, they were Guinness men through and through.

"Actually, the party is here because you *are* invited, so," Lochlan gestured to the three glasses, "you need to pour one for yourself. We thought we'd lift a glass in honor of Fergus's fatherhood. Celebrating the newest addition to the Collins family with wings and beer."

Padraig grabbed a glass for himself. "An excellent idea."

Fergus's wife, Aubrey, had delivered a healthy baby girl this morning after a long night of labor. Fergus had texted several middle-of-the-night updates, clearly going out of his mind with worry for his wife, despite the reassurances of every male in the family who'd already walked this path that she and the baby would be just fine.

According to the new dad in his last text—which was accompanied by a picture of the tiny baby in Aubrey's arms—Sophie Grace Collins had entered the world kicking and screaming at the ass crack of dawn. And there was no question Fergus was already head over heels in love with his precious daughter.

Lochlan lifted his glass. "To Fergus, who will never enjoy another peaceful night's sleep in his life. Poor bastard."

"Poor bastard," Oliver, Finn, and Padraig all chimed in, chuckling before taking a sip of their beer. For a few minutes, the four of them dug into the plate of wings, dipping them in ranch, while talking sports.

Then Finn glanced down toward Emmy's end of the bar. "Where's Em?"

"Doctor's office. Annual physical. She's coming here to write afterwards."

"Which explains that shit-eating grin of yours," Oliver said, turning the conversation around to Padraig. "I assume this means things are going good?"

Padraig didn't even bother to play it cool. "Things are amazing. Seriously. Unbelievably great. We've spent every single night together since the soft opening of the pub."

"I thought I recognized that oversexed glow," Finn joked.

"Jealous?" Padraig teased.

"I live with my boyfriend *and* my girlfriend, so I'll let you figure out the answer to that on your own," Finn replied, making it perfectly clear he was just as oversexed.

Lochlan groaned. "You guys are going to have to take it easy on me with the sex talk. I've got a toddler going through a phase. Wyatt starts out in his bed every night, but by midnight, he's crawling in between me and May. And you know my wife. May has now read every article in the world about 'the family bed,'" Lochlan said, finger-quoting the last. "I'm starting to worry I won't get laid again until Wyatt starts high school."

They all laughed as Oliver leaned toward Lochlan, bumping his shoulder against his older cousin's. "So I guess now is a bad time for me to say I'm in the same happy boat as Finn. Only better—honeymoon phase and all that."

Oliver had been dating his girlfriend, Erin, for a year and a half, but over the holidays, their "couple" status shifted to "throuple" as they both fell head over heels for Oliver's best friend, Gavin, as well. Oliver definitely had that "new car" smell when it came to his change in relationship status, his grin a permanent fixture on his face these days.

Lochlan narrowed his eyes. "Asshole," he muttered good-naturedly. Then he turned his gaze back to Padraig. "I have to admit, I'm happy for you, cuz. Really happy."

Padraig smiled at Lochlan's heartfelt comment. He knew how much his family had worried about him over the past few years. He'd gone to a dark place after Mia died, and it had taken him a long time to find his way back. Emmy—and his family—had been his guides, and he was certain that without them, he'd still be trapped in the darkness.

"Thanks, Lochlan. I can't believe how easily we've made the transition from just friends to a couple. Nothing has been hard work—everything's coming so naturally. It's like she was made for me. We've been alternating between her place and mine every night, and we've introduced Seamus to her cats. Luna hides under the bed whenever my crazy mutt is there, but I think she'll warm up to him. Neville is completely indifferent, which seems to be that cat's attitude about everything."

"Wow. Introduction of pets. This *is* serious," Lochlan said with a chuckle. "A regular blended family."

Padraig took another swig of his Guinness. "I know you're joking, but to be honest, that's exactly what it feels like. I've been thinking it's probably silly for Em and me to keep the two apartments when we're together every night. I spent the morning debating with myself over which place we should keep. Mine is closer to the pub, but hers is a bit bigger."

"Wait a minute," Finn said, holding his hand up in a stop motion. "You're thinking about moving in together?"

"Of course. Why wouldn't we?"

Oliver frowned. "Maybe because your relationship is all of two weeks old."

Padraig rolled his eyes. "We've been dating two weeks, but we've been friends a lot longer. This isn't a new relationship."

Finn tilted his head. "Actually, it is. Weren't you the guy who proclaimed on Christmas Eve that he wasn't ready to date? You've only just turned the corner and jumped back into the dating scene. Why don't you enjoy that for a little while before rushing to the next part?"

Padraig wasn't sure what to make of his cousins

attempting to slow down his relationship, but it was obvious from Lochlan and Oliver's faces, they agreed with Finn.

He knew they were crazy about Emmy. And they'd all—at some point in the past year—tried to convince him to start dating again, so this advice seemed in direct contrast to everything they'd said before.

"I'm not sure it matters how fast or slow we go. I know how I feel about her. I'm all in—and I want it all. Marriage, babies, the whole shebang."

The desire for children had appeared just that morning, when Fergus had texted the picture of Sophie in Aubrey's arms. Padraig had shown it to Emmy, and as she oohed and ahhed over the tiny baby, Padraig had imagined it was her with *their* child in her arms. The second his mind conjured the image, he'd been unable to unsee it. He wanted to be a father, and he wanted Emmy to be the mother of his children, telling them the stories about her beloved rocks.

"Marriage?" Oliver said. At the same time Lochlan said, "Babies?"

"I'm thirty-four years old, guys. I know what I want, and I'm not getting any younger."

"You say thirty-four like it's ancient," Finn said. "I can assure you, it's not."

"Maybe not, but why would I drag my feet? The end result is going to be the same. It's the Collins curse," he said with a grin. "It struck me twice."

Lochlan rubbed his chin, sighing heavily.

"You have something to say?" Padraig asked, aware that Lochlan obviously had something on his mind, something he was apparently hesitant to bring up.

"I understand how you feel, Paddy," Lochlan said. "I really do. If you'll recall, I fell fast and hard for May. And I remember a wise man telling me to slow down."

Padraig grimaced, recalling the late-night phone call from Lochlan when his cousin realized he'd fallen in love with his new personal assistant. Padraig had issued the advice, teasing Lochlan that if he confessed his undying love after just a few short weeks, May would run for the hills. The thing was... Lochlan hadn't taken the advice.

"I did say that. And May was pregnant within a month, and you were married a few months after that, so..." Padraig waved his hand as if to say he rested his case.

"You're right. Absolutely right. But...do you think maybe you're rushing things with Emmy because of your relationship with Mia?"

Padraig frowned. "What do you mean?"

"Paddy, you and Mia lived your lives in fast-forward because you didn't have a choice. And I'm not saying that was wrong. Not at all. What the two of you shared, the way your relationship evolved, it was right for both of you. It had to happen that way because..." Lochlan didn't add the last part, didn't mention they'd rushed through every facet of their relationship because they'd known their time together would be short. He didn't say it because he didn't have to.

"I hear you, but——"

"No." Lochlan raised his hand. "No buts. You don't have to rush things with Emmy. You can take your time and enjoy every single aspect of your relationship with her. You don't have to do everything yesterday."

"Lochlan, you of all people should know how hard it is to tap on the brakes when every fiber of your being is telling you this is it, she's the one."

Lochlan looked at Oliver and Finn. "I'm tapping out. He's right. I'm probably not the best one to make this argument. You two try to talk some sense into him."

Finn gave him a rueful grin. "I agree with Lochlan. You're

not living on borrowed time this time around, Paddy. Stop and smell the roses. And we're not saying you have to drag your feet for years. But maybe enjoy the novelty of a new relationship, take your time and date for a few months."

Oliver chimed in as well. "It's obvious you and Emmy are made for each other, and neither of you is going anywhere, so why not savor it? Spend some time getting to discover all the bits and pieces of each other. That's what I've been doing with Gavin and Erin the past few months, and it's been awesome. Every single day, we peel off another layer and fall more in love. We know where we're headed and what we want, but we're not racing to the next part. We're strolling there, hand in hand."

"Plus," Finn started, "this is your first relationship since Mia's death. I get that it's great, but I think you should take some time—for Emmy's sake *and* for yours—to be really sure. It's good now, but...well...there could be some bumps down the road, things you're not expecting, things you'll have to work through together."

"Emmy's not going anywhere, Paddy," Lochlan added, reassuringly. "Just remember. You have time. Lots of time."

Padraig appreciated their advice, but he still struggled to accept it. "Okay. I'll think about what you've said."

"Good." Lochlan reached for a wipe, so Finn made a grab for the last wing on the plate.

"Whoa, whoa, whoa," Lochlan said. "What are you doing?" he asked Finn.

"You reached for a wipe," Finn said, taking a big bite of the wing.

"So?" Lochlan pressed.

"So..." Finn drawled. "You reach for a wipe, it means you're done."

Lochlan scowled. "That's beside the point."

Finn chuckled. "Um, no. That *is* the point."

"Count the bones on your plate," Lochlan insisted.

Finn looked down. "Seven."

"That's right. You've got seven bones there. I've got five, which proves you've already had more than your share. I was entitled to the rhetorical offer."

Oliver snorted. "Rhetorical offer?"

"Yes," Lochlan said. "Rhetorical offer. Finn should have asked me if I wanted the last wing. Hell, he should have asked all of us."

"You reached for a wipe!" Finn said loudly. "Ollie and Paddy had already wiped. The issue of the last wing was solved. No offer necessary."

"If we'd been even or you'd had fewer wings, I might be able to support that, Finn, but the fact is we were all owed a rhetorical offer."

Finn rolled his eyes and fake-sneezed the word "bullshit."

"It's simple wing etiquette," Lochlan insisted while Padraig and Oliver cracked up. Battles like these were a dime a dozen in their family, and there were times Padraig was sorry his cousin Fiona wasn't around more often. A sitcom writer in Hollywood, she would have loved the wing argument, and he didn't doubt she would have written it into a scene on her show, *Wild Winters*. He'd have to remember to call her later to repeat it.

They were still laughing when the bell over the front door rang and Emmy walked in.

She smiled at him and his cousins as she approached them. "Looks like this is a happy happy hour," she said.

Finn jerked his thumb toward Lochlan. "It was until this one started making up rules for the wings."

Emmy took in the empty platter, then looked at Padraig. "Do I want to know?"

He laughed. "I'll tell you later. Probably best you get the rundown so you don't screw up in the future."

She rolled her eyes, amused. "So what's the occasion?"

"Drinking a Guinness in honor of the new father, Fergus."

"That's so nice of you guys." Emmy lifted a small bag in her hand. "I actually just popped into that little boutique across the street, the one with all the adorable baby clothes." She pulled out a cute little pink dress and held it up. "How sweet is this?" she asked. "I thought we could get a congratulations card, Paddy, and run it by the hospital to them in the morning."

"That sounds great. Thanks so much for thinking of it," Padraig said, touched by Emmy's thoughtfulness and grateful that she loved his family as much as he did. He also liked the idea of them buying gifts that were from both of them.

"Well," Lochlan said, rising after downing the last of his beer. "That's it for me. Promised May I'd hit the mall with the family before dinner. Jenny and Chloe need new winter coats. Those girls are growing like weeds."

May had assumed custody of her nieces after her brother and his wife were killed in a car accident. Since then, she and Lochlan had officially adopted both of the girls.

Everyone said their goodbyes and he left.

"Want to see the progress Justin and Killian have made on the apartment, Finn?" Oliver asked. "Don't think you've seen it since the fire."

"I'd love to." Finn and Oliver rose as well, heading for the staircase at the back of the pub that led to the Collins Dorm. Oliver, Erin, and Gavin hoped to be able to move back into the apartment soon, planning to make it their forever home, raising their family there just as Pop Pop and Sunday had before them.

"How was the doctor?" Padraig asked Emmy when they were alone.

She shrugged. "Fine."

"Just fine?"

"I don't think any woman is going to rave about how much fun she had getting a pap smear."

Padraig feigned a horrified face at her use of the words *pap smear*. "Glass of wine?"

"Well, I have been sitting here all of three minutes..." she teased, reaching into her bag to retrieve her laptop case.

"How's the book coming along?" he asked, wiggling his eyebrows suggestively. "Need to do any more research?"

Emmy laughed. "I think it's safe to say you and I have done enough research for the next twenty books."

"Is that all? Damn. We better get busy." Padraig poured her wine and slid it across the counter to her. "I should warn you. Aunt Riley has been on the lookout for you. She and Bubbles have decided they want to have a book club meeting or party or something, with you as their featured guest author."

"Oh my God. Did you have to tell every single member of your family my pen name?" Her grin let him know she wasn't as annoyed as she pretended.

"Couldn't exactly claim the betting pool money without the proof. And it was a big pot. Kelli is trying to say I had an unfair advantage, but that's just because she's a sore loser."

"Guess I know what book Bubbles and Riley want to talk about at their book club meeting."

Padraig chuckled. "The Vegas one."

Emmy glanced toward Sunday's Side and the kitchen. "I hope your aunt wasn't too upset by that book. I mean...that one was a little too true to life. The story of how Riley and

Aaron met Bubbles, and how they eloped in Vegas, was just too good not to write down."

"Bubbles swears it's like you were there with them. And Riley absolutely loves it. She's told every single customer who's walked into the restaurant this week that they should read it. If you had a fan club, Riley would already be the president."

"Maybe I should hire your aunt to be my publicist," Emmy joked.

"The family texts this week have been nothing but book talk, everyone pointing out parts that sound just like them or their romances. They're having a ball."

"I'm glad no one is upset," she admitted.

"Upset? Hell no. Emmy, you create the best characters, people you can really root for. And the sex scenes...Jesus, woman. If I'd known you'd been sitting right across this counter the past two years writing that?! Damn. I don't know what I would have done."

"Will it overinflate your ego if I say you inspired a lot of those scenes?"

"I think my ego is okay," Padraig teased, leaning over the counter to get closer to her and lowering his voice. "But something else is definitely overinflated at the moment. Think I could entice you into joining me for a quickie in the storage closet?"

Emmy shook her head. "Nope. No lock, remember?"

"Heartless woman," Padraig said, winking, then walking away when someone at the other end of the bar asked for a refill.

Emmy finished setting up her laptop and started tapping away at the keys, something Padraig had watched her do a million times before. Now that he'd had a chance to read her books, he was even more in awe of her. He'd always been curious how she was able to write in a crowded, noisy pub, but it was apparent that it was the people and this place that fed her imagination.

He'd already worked his way through several of her books, which was saying something, considering he hadn't read a book in his life that hadn't been assigned in school. And even for half of those, he'd found CliffsNotes to avoid actually cracking open the book.

A few nights ago, they'd taken on roles from the BDSM book she was currently writing, with him assuming the part of the hero, a billionaire Dom. Emmy was a natural submissive—something he couldn't think about without getting a hard-on.

By the time they'd fallen asleep, physically exhausted, they'd had sex on the floor of her living room with her on her hands and knees in front of him as he'd spanked her and fucked her at the same time, then again in the bedroom, where he'd bound her spread eagle and withheld her orgasm for nearly an hour—then once more in the bathtub, with her straddling his hips, riding him. All three times they'd remained in character, the night so sexually charged and exciting, he couldn't wait to do it all over again.

"What's the plan for tonight?" he asked after he'd made his rounds of the patrons, refilling drinks.

"I thought I'd write here until dinnertime and eat with you. Then I need to do some laundry, so do you mind if we stay at my place tonight? I can swing by your apartment to get Seamus so you can come straight over after work."

He nodded, recalling his conversation with his cousins. They'd told him to take his time, not to rush to the next part, but he couldn't make himself follow that advice. "You know, I've been thinking about our apartment situation."

Emmy glanced up from her computer. "We have a situation?"

He grinned. "We have two. What if we only had one?"

"You want to move in together?"

Padraig tried to read the tone in her voice, but he was struggling. "We've spent every night together since the soft opening of the pub, and I don't see that changing in the near future. No, strike the word near. I don't see it changing period."

Emmy gave him a sweet smile. "I like the sound of that. But, Paddy, we've only been dating for a couple of weeks. Doesn't it seem sort of soon to start talking about moving in? You haven't had time to discover all my bad habits," she joked.

"Like?" he prompted.

"I never reuse towels, so I always have a pile of them in the corner of the bathroom. It's a problem."

Padraig laughed. "I think I can deal with that, if you can handle the fact that I tend to leave big globs of toothpaste in the bathroom sink."

Emmy crinkled her nose. "Ew. Gross. That might actually be a deal breaker." Then she continued, "There will always be at least five empty glasses or water bottles on my nightstand. *At least*," she stressed. "Usually it's way more."

Padraig was getting into the spirit of the game and hoping he was convincing Emmy that moving in together would be okay. "I'm the messiest coffee maker in the world. Always leave grounds around the pot on the kitchen counter."

"Luna gets a ridiculous amount of hairballs, so it's not unusual to wake up to cat puke somewhere in the apartment. And believe me, you'll step in it barefoot before you'll ever see it. It's disgusting."

"Seamus snores. Loudly."

"I've already discovered that," she countered. "He also hogs the covers."

"None of this is bad, Emmy. I like having someone to eat breakfast and dinner with, someone to fight over the remote with at night, someone there keeping the bed warm when I get home after a late night here at the pub. I've lived alone the past three years. These past two weeks with you have been...God...really fucking good."

Her cheeks flushed pink with pleasure. "They've been good for me too."

"So why wait?"

Emmy shrugged, and he could see she wasn't totally convinced. "Let me think about it?"

He nodded, tempted to push the issue, but Lochlan and Finn's words drifted back to him, so he held his tongue. "Sure. Take some time," he said.

Unfortunately, the second he agreed to wait, he felt a pressure on his chest...and he couldn't shake the feeling that time wasn't a luxury they had. The sand in the hourglass was flowing too quickly for his peace of mind.

Shit. His cousins were right. Logically, he knew they *did* have time—all the time in the world—but his head couldn't convince his heart of that.

No matter how hard he tried.

❧ 10 ❧

Emmy smiled as Sunnie joined her at a booth in the pub. She'd asked her friend to meet her for a quick chat after her shift at the hospital. The two of them ordered iced teas, since Sunnie was pregnant and margaritas were typically reserved for girls' night. Emmy needed some medical advice, and Sunnie, who worked as a nurse at Johns Hopkins, felt like the best person to talk to.

She had picked today because Padraig wasn't manning the bar. His father, Tris, was. Padraig and a bunch of the Collins men were helping Oliver, Erin, and Gavin move some of their furniture back into the renovated apartment above the pub.

She'd wanted to have this conversation in private, her nervousness off the charts at the moment.

"Thanks so much for stopping by, especially after a shift. I'm sure you're anxious to get home."

Sunnie waved her off, insisting she was fine. Sunnie was always a bundle of energy and she glowed with her pregnancy. "I'm fine. If I time it right, I'll be just late enough that Landon has to make dinner. Besides, I'd already told Mom I was stopping by to borrow a book." Sunnie winked, making it clear she and Riley were swapping Emmy's romance novels.

Emmy rolled her eyes. "I swear to God I've seen a spike in sales, and I'm convinced it's solely because of your family. You know, I would give you all the books. You don't have to buy them."

"Don't be silly. We love being able to support you, and your books rock. The whole family is hooked. Landon said Miguel has a bunch of guys at the precinct reading them now too."

"Oh my God."

Sunnie laughed. "Bubbles bought every single one of them in one fell swoop. She thinks they all need to be made into movies—she actually called Fiona last night to see who she needed to pitch them to in Hollywood—and, of course, she wants to play herself. I swear she's found herself in at least ten of the books already."

Emmy sighed. "She's probably not wrong. Bubbles is just too funny not to include."

"Yeah, well, be prepared the next time you see her because she's got all sorts of plans for 'her book,' the one where she's the heroine. Has decided she wants her story to be one of those reverse harem things where she's got four men worshipping her. She's actually started jotting down some notes."

"Shit," Emmy muttered, prompting Sunnie to laugh even harder.

"So what's up? You said you needed advice."

Emmy reached into her purse and pulled out the letter she'd received from the doctor's office a couple of days earlier. The results of her pap smear had come back abnormal, and the doctor wanted to do a second test.

Sunnie scanned the letter, then mercifully shrugged, clearly unconcerned. Emmy had immediately done a bit of research online after reading the results, and she'd discovered that false positives were common. Sunnie's casual response seemed to support that information.

"You've only had the one pap smear, right?" Sunnie asked.

Emmy nodded.

"Then go back for the second. And don't worry yet. It's waaaay too early to worry. It's either a false positive or, if not, you could have a slight infection or something. The chance that it's cancer is minimal. Like, seriously minimal."

"Okay. That's good to know."

Sunnie studied her face for a moment. "But that's not really what you wanted to know, is it? I mean, a quick Google search would have told you that."

Emmy sighed. "That's not all I wanted to talk about, no."

"Did you tell Paddy about it?" Sunnie asked. "Oh my God. Did he freak out?"

Emmy hesitated for a moment, then shook her head. "No. I didn't tell him. I wanted to wait until I got the results of the second pap smear."

"I think that's a good idea."

Emmy breathed a sigh of relief. In addition to the medical information, she'd been hoping for Sunnie's reassurance over not telling Padraig. She knew what he'd gone through with Mia, and there was no way in hell she wanted to cause him a minute of worry if she could spare him. Especially since there was a chance this abnormal pap smear result was a false positive.

"You do? Really?" Emmy pressed. She'd been stressed out the last two days, less about the results and more about Padraig's *reaction* to the results.

"Yeah, I do. Waiting is prudent. I mean...after what Paddy went through with Mia."

"That's what I was thinking," Emmy said.

"When's your second test?" Sunnie asked.

"Tomorrow."

"Excellent. So you don't have too long to worry about it. And if this one comes back negative..." Sunnie paused.

"You don't think I should tell Paddy at all, do you?" Emmy asked, grateful for her friend's advice.

Sunnie had been there during Padraig's marriage to Mia. His cousin had an insight into Padraig that Emmy didn't have. All Emmy knew of Padraig and Mia's relationship was secondhand stories, from Padraig and from others. Hearing things after the fact was different from having a front-row seat, so she really didn't know how this news might impact him. If he'd take it in stride or if he'd—as Sunnie said—freak out.

Sunnie shrugged. "I don't think you should tell him. I mean, if it's negative, then what is there to tell? If it had been a negative this time, would you have told him about it?"

Emmy shook her head. "No. I wouldn't have even thought about it. It's just a routine physical. But do you think this is lying through omission? This relationship between me and Paddy is new, and I don't want to screw things up, Sunnie. So is it better to save him from the hurt and worry this might cause or come clean about all of it?"

Sunnie didn't respond right away, taking her time to think, which Emmy respected. "Tell him after you get the results from the second test. Regardless of what they are. You need to be able to talk to him about stuff like this. It's part of being a couple. I just want you to be prepared because I really don't know how he'll respond."

Emmy nodded. "Okay. I will. And you're right, he and I do need to talk about it. So...after the second test, I'm coming clean. Thanks, Sunnie. I really appreciate it."

"What's going on here?" Padraig said, walking over to their table, a large box labeled "dishes" in his hands.

Emmy panicked briefly, wondering if he'd heard anything they were talking about.

"I came to borrow a spicy romance novel from Mom," Sunnie said, quickly diverting Padraig's attention while Emmy hastily shoved the letter from the doctor back into her purse. "Ran into the author on my way to the kitchen."

Padraig chuckled and rested the box, which appeared heavy, on the edge of their table.

"You guys need any help?" Emmy offered.

"Naw. We've moved all we planned to. Just the heavy shit today—furniture, books, dishes. Erin, Oliver, and Gavin said they can handle the lighter things, like their clothes, sheets, towels. Truth is, they don't have a whole lot of stuff. Oliver and Gavin lost most of their possessions in the fire. Good thing Erin had her own apartment full of furniture they can move over here."

"Glad you got it all moved before the storm hits," Sunnie mused, glancing over her shoulder toward the large glass window. Dark storm clouds obscured the sky, the forecast calling for heavy rains late in the afternoon and throughout the evening. "Guess I should leave before it starts raining, but..." Sunnie glanced at the time on her phone. "Dammit. Looks like I'm going to have to help make dinner," she said, sighing dramatically.

"I'm going to head home now too," Emmy said to Padraig. "Going to make spaghetti for dinner and the sauce is better if it simmers for a while. I'll take care of Seamus when I get there so we're not walking him in a storm later."

Padraig bent down and gave her a quick kiss on the cheek. "Thanks, sweetheart." Then he looked around the pub. "I know I'm off tonight, but I might stick around here a little while, once I take this box upstairs. I think I should give Dad a hand. Not sure why the pub is so busy on a Thursday night."

"Your dad said the same thing when I walked in," Emmy admitted. "Apparently there's some big conference in town and the accountants found the pub. Sunday's Side is slammed too."

Padraig frowned. "Let me run this upstairs. I'm going to pitch in here until the rush is over. See you at home later."

Emmy smiled as he hefted the box and headed to the apartment above. Padraig loved the pub and took pride in the business his family ran.

She and Sunnie settled up their tab and said their good-byes to Tris before Padraig reappeared, so Emmy walked out with Sunnie. "Thanks again for your advice," Emmy said.

"Any time."

Sunnie got into her car while Emmy hurriedly walked down the block toward her apartment. The black storm clouds overhead, heavy with rain, reflected her mood, and she shivered as a feeling of impending doom passed through her. Despite Sunnie's reassurances, keeping a secret like this from Padraig rubbed against the grain, even though she knew it was for the best.

Please let the next test be okay, she silently prayed.

Padraig came back downstairs, then stepped behind the bar. He took off his jacket, put on an apron, and grabbed a washcloth. "I'll bus some tables," he offered, while his dad hustled to make drinks for a large group who'd just come in.

"Thanks," Dad said. "I considered calling you a few minutes ago. Glad you're here. I could use the extra help."

"No problem."

Padraig cleared several tables before heading to the booth

Emmy and Sunnie had just vacated. He wiped the surface, then noticed a piece of paper on one of the seats. Picking it up, he opened the letter, seeing Emmy's name on top. The letterhead revealed it was from her doctor's office, and he recalled the letter showing up in the mail a couple days earlier. It must have fallen out of her purse. He shoved it into his pocket to return to her later.

For the next hour or so, he and his dad hustled to serve the crowd. Once it started to thin out, his dad assured him he could handle things for the rest of the night. The storm still hadn't started, but given the even-darker clouds, Padraig was fairly certain he wasn't going to make it to Emmy's without getting wet. Luckily, he kept an umbrella behind the bar.

He put on his jacket, then reached into the pocket of his jeans to make sure he had his keys. He pulled out the folded-up letter from Emmy's doctor along with his keys, intent on moving both to his jacket pocket. Curious, he flipped it open and his eyes landed on a word he hadn't noticed before.

Abnormal.

He skimmed the letter as he walked out of the pub, forgetting all about the umbrella. Stopping under the awning, he read the lab results more carefully.

The results of Emmy's pap smear were abnormal. There was a note from her doctor telling her he wanted to schedule a second one.

The doctor had written that a positive test could indicate cervical cancer.

Suddenly, Padraig suspected Sunnie really hadn't come to the pub just to grab a book. She'd been dressed in her scrubs, so it had been the end of her shift. Had Emmy asked to meet with her?

Padraig leaned against the wall of the pub, the words

cervical cancer reverberating in his brain like a bomb had been detonated.

He tried to suck in a deep breath, but his lungs were constricted, tight. He rubbed his chest with his palm, worried he might be having a heart attack. Actually, he hoped he was. That would sure as fuck be preferable to discovering Emmy had...

Cancer.

It couldn't be.

He closed his eyes, trying to block out the word, but it kept repeating itself, playing on a loop in his mind.

Cancer. Cancer. Cancer.

And with every repetition came a sharp pain in his chest as excruciating, gut-wrenching fear cut through him like a blade. Mia's face flashed in his mind, the tears she'd fought so hard to hold back as she told him she was dying. He couldn't hear those again. Not from Emmy.

Jesus. It felt as if he were being struck by lightning over and over, but the storm hadn't started yet.

Emmy couldn't be sick. He'd just seen her. She was the picture of health. Wouldn't he know if...

No. He wouldn't.

He recalled that initial night with Mia, when she'd come into the pub after learning about the brain tumor. She hadn't looked sick then. The disease was too insidious, too evil. It refused to show its ugly fucking face, preferring to strike a healthy, beautiful woman silently at first, until...

No. He couldn't think about that. Couldn't...lose Emmy that same way. He wasn't strong enough to live in a world where she didn't exist.

Padraig ran his fingers through his hair roughly, yanking it hard, as if that might somehow erase the word.

Cancer.

His hands started to tremble as he looked down at the letter crumpled in his fist. Emmy had known about these test results for two days. Why hadn't she told him?

Why?

He knew why.

Deep down, he knew.

And if he was in a reasonable state of mind—rather than in the throes of a brutal panic attack—he'd probably even understand.

But right now, he didn't. He really fucking didn't.

She knew. And she didn't tell him.

Cancer.

"Fuck," he muttered, thrashing his head back and forth, desperate to find some way to force that fucking word out of his thoughts forever. Why wouldn't it just shut up?!

"Shut up!" he shouted into the night.

He quickly jogged down the block, away from the pub, when the door opened and someone started to walk out. He couldn't see anyone, couldn't talk to anyone.

The sound of voices he didn't recognize drifted away from him, mercifully growing softer as whoever it was walked the opposite direction.

When he reached the corner, a wave of nausea caught him completely off guard. He bent at the waist, his hands on his knees as he retched, dry-heaving, choking on a knowledge he didn't want to face.

I can't do this again.

He replayed those words over and over and over as he swallowed down the bile and forced himself to stand upright. Raindrops splattered his face. He realized belatedly that the rain had finally started, but he barely felt it, his body chilled from the inside out, ice coursing through his veins.

Padraig drifted farther down the street with no direction in mind. He just needed to walk, to move. If he stopped...

I can't do this again.

Too many memories started pounding inside his brain, each one slicing through him deeper and deeper.

The nose bleeds, the seizures, the headaches, the countless medications with shitty side effects, the hours spent in doctors' offices and the hospital. Mia kept hoping against hope for a miracle. He'd done the same. Kept thinking it was all a nightmare they'd wake up from. Then she went to sleep forever, and...now he was plunged back into the same horrifying nightmare.

There'd been no miracle.

Only pain. Fear. Misery. Uncertainty. Sadness.

God no. Please! He didn't want to see it again, didn't want to remember.

Then he realized this time, it wasn't Mia he saw bent over the toilet, throwing up as a migraine ravaged her.

It was Emmy.

Tears streamed down his face as he saw himself lying next to Emmy in a hospital bed, holding her hand, the only sound that goddamned horrible, rasping breathing, as she took one last look at him and...

I can't do this again.

"No," he said aloud, barely able to hear his own voice over the driving rain. It was beating down on him hard now, thunder rumbling in the distance. "No. No. No."

Glancing up, Padraig realized he was standing outside Emmy's building. He looked up and saw the light in her window. She'd have spaghetti sauce simmering in a pot on the stove, the television playing in the background. She'd probably be watching one of those cooking competition shows —*Chopped* or *Crime Scene Kitchen* or some silly shit like that.

Seamus would be dogging her every step, the sweet mutt completely devoted to her.

Just like Mia.

Padraig sucked in a deep breath, stiffened his spine, and forced himself to walk inside.

I can't do this again.

Emmy heard the knock on the door just as she turned on a pot of water to boil.

She grinned as she opened it. "Did you forget your key?" she asked before her gaze landed on Padraig. "Oh my God. You're drenched. Where's your umbrella?"

Padraig didn't speak as he entered. He only took a few steps inside before shutting the door behind him.

"Let me grab you a towel," she said, turning to head to the bathroom.

Padraig reached out and grasped her wrist, halting her. "No."

"Paddy. You're going to catch your death of cold if you don't dry off. Take off your clothes and I'll run to the bedroom for some dry things for you."

Both of them now had a drawer in each other's apartments filled with spare clothing. While she'd pushed off his suggestion that they move in together, there was no denying they were getting there on their own even without further discussion.

He retained his grip on her wrist, then lifted his other hand, revealing a soggy piece of paper. "Were you going to tell me about this?"

Emmy, confused, took the paper from him, and felt a stabbing pierce in her chest when she realized it was the letter from the doctor. "Where did you—"

"It was on the seat of the booth where you were sitting." His tone was cold, angry.

"It must have fallen out of my purse," she said stupidly, as she struggled for some way to explain.

"Were you going to tell me?" he repeated.

She nodded. "I was. After the second test. I swear. I talked to Sunnie about it today. She said false positives are very common. Thirty-five percent are typically wrong. I googled it."

Padraig's face appeared to be carved in stone. She'd never seen him so still, so stiff. "Do you feel okay? Are you alright...physically?" he asked, with no inflection, no emotion.

His concerned questions might have touched her if it didn't seem like he was a stranger. She didn't recognize this cold, detached man, and it scared her. "I feel fine."

"I thought the check was an annual physical. Did you go because you knew something was wrong?"

"God no! It *was* just a checkup. I'm sorry I didn't tell you, but I wanted to wait. Until I got the results of the second test. According to the medical websites I looked at, less than one percent of people who have this test actually have..." She hesitated.

"Say it."

She didn't want to. She really didn't.

"Say it, Emmy."

"Cervical cancer," she finished.

Padraig winced when she said the words, but he didn't respond, his silence deafening.

"I should have told you. I just—"

"You just what?" he asked woodenly.

Emmy's heart was racing. It felt like nothing she said was helping or setting his mind at ease. She was helpless to fix what she'd broken. But God, she wanted to fix it. "I didn't want to worry you. After everything...you've been through."

She watched him swallow heavily, his Adam's apple moving slowly, as if there was something lodged in his throat. She knew the feeling.

"Emmy. When I read those test results, it felt like I'd been punched in the gut, like someone had swung a sledgehammer at me."

She blinked rapidly, trying to stem the tears suddenly filling her eyes. "I'm so sorry. Please, you have to believe me. I wouldn't hide something from you if...I just wanted to wait until..."

"I understand why you didn't tell me."

It was obvious that while Padraig might understand the reasons for her silence, he sure as hell didn't accept them.

"I made a mistake," she started, but Padraig wasn't listening to her.

He was shaking his head slowly, back and forth, his gaze far away. "I know why you didn't say anything, but when I read those words, the idea...that you might have..." He swallowed deeply again, his voice gruff, suddenly hoarse with emotion.

Emmy noticed the puffiness around his eyes. She'd attributed it to the rain, but now she wasn't so sure. Had he been crying?

The thought triggered her own sorrow, and she was powerless to stop the tears now streaming down her cheeks.

She tried to wipe them away, but Padraig wasn't looking at her, didn't notice her distress, too lost in his own pain.

"I stood outside and...replayed it all."

"Replayed what?" she asked, praying to God it wasn't what she imagined.

"Mia," he whispered.

"No," she said softly. "No, Paddy. That's why I didn't want—"

He was still lost to her, still too deep in his own thoughts. "Only this time, it wasn't her. It was you. Your face, your pain. Your death."

Emmy clutched her neck, fighting hard to swallow, her throat closed. It was hard to breathe with her tears choking her. "Please, Paddy. Everything is fine. I'm fine."

For the first time, his eyes flashed with anger, his gaze singeing her. "It's not fine! None of this is *fine*!"

She jumped, startled by the vehemence behind his words. She'd never heard him so angry. Emmy tried once more to talk him off the ledge, even though she knew it was hopeless. "Let's just wait for the results of the second test." She heard the pleading, desperate tone in her voice, but she didn't know what else to say, how to stave off what was coming. It was as if she was standing on the tracks, facing down the train but helpless to step out of its path.

"I thought I could do this, Emmy. I thought..."

"Please," she said again, terrified to hear what he might say next. "Please don't."

He was silent as he held her gaze, his eyes awash with anguish and desolation. She recognized the look from the reflection she'd seen in the mirror right after her mother—and then her father—died.

"You're leaving." She didn't pose it as a question. She didn't have to.

He stared at her for a long time. So long, she wasn't sure he'd speak again.

Finally—horribly—he said, "I need time."

It was on the tip of her tongue to ask him what he needed time for. He already knew what he was going to do. But she held her peace.

"I need time to..."

He didn't finish. Because like her, he knew what was coming too. He just wasn't ready to say it.

She tried to nod, fought like the devil to make her head go up, then down again...because she got it. Or at least the still-broken part of her that had spent years grieving her beloved parents did.

The rest of her didn't understand at all. Those parts were tattered, ripped to shreds, dying a million deaths.

The irony of it was rich.

He couldn't be *with* her.

She couldn't be *without* him.

"Please," she whispered once more, her denial running strong, refusing to believe what was coming. This couldn't be happening. "Paddy, I love you."

Neither of them had said those words yet. They'd known they were there, so she wasn't sure why they'd gone unspoken until now.

He closed his eyes, his head bent, as if her words physically hurt him.

"I'm sorry, Emmy. So sorry." He spoke so quietly, she almost didn't hear him, especially when a crack of thunder pierced the night.

She forced a sad smile, hating that she couldn't hide her tears, that she couldn't make this easier for either of them.

She was shattered.

Destroyed.

Instead, she offered him what little comfort she could manage.

"I know," she said. "I know you are."

Padraig held her gaze for a second longer, then he looked away, reaching for Seamus's leash. He clipped it onto the dog's collar and then...he left.

Without another word.

Not even goodbye.

PADRAIG WALKED BACK TO HIS APARTMENT, NUMBNESS setting in. The rain had stopped briefly, a temporary reprieve. The clouds overhead weren't finished yet and he expected another deluge any minute.

His brain had gone blank, every thought, fear, emotion muted. All he could see was Emmy's face as he walked away. As he broke her heart.

He tried to convince himself it was better this way. That he'd made the right decision, the smart one. She should understand after all. He wasn't the only one who'd loved and lost, who understood the unbearable pain of grief.

He couldn't give her what she wanted, what she needed, so he'd set her free. Free so that she could find the love, the life, she deserved, if she...

While he...

"Fuck," he muttered. He should never have asked her out, given in to...all these feelings. Love came with too high a price tag. He'd paid it once and it had bankrupted him. He wouldn't go through that again.

No. He'd done the right thing. This was the right thing.

Unfortunately, that self-assurance only lasted until he reached the door of his apartment, then the pain set back in, crippling him. Seamus, typically energetic, seemed to feed from his depression. The dog was quiet, sitting next to him as Padraig struggled to withdraw his keys from the pocket of his wet jeans.

Once he retrieved them, he unlocked the door and walked in, unclipping Seamus from the leash. He shut the door behind him, then fell back against it, as the barrage of emotions he'd been holding at bay collapsed down on him, an avalanche of agony.

He slid down the door until his ass hit the floor. He rested his elbows on his knees, scrubbing his eyes with the palms of his hands, trying to beat back the tears.

"Emmy," he whispered miserably to the empty room.

He recalled the last time he'd been on his ass by this door, the memory provoking a shadow of a smile.

He'd gotten extremely inebriated at his family's Halloween party the year before last. Baltimore had been submerged in darkness, thanks to a blackout, and Sunnie had proposed some silly game that involved tequila. A lot of tequila.

Padraig had over-imbibed, upset over nearly losing Seamus in the park earlier in the day and overwhelmed with loneliness. His depression over the past three years seemed to ebb and flow like the tide—sometimes nonexistent, other times overwhelming. The holidays the first year after Mia's death had been brutal, Padraig lost in a downward spiral from Halloween to St. Patrick's Day.

So when Halloween arrived again the next year, and he'd felt himself being swallowed by the void, he'd been helpless to climb out, resigning himself to months of exhaustion and misery. That night had been a bad one for him, and if he hadn't agreed to a partner costume with Emmy, he probably would have sent his regrets and stayed home. Instead, he'd gone and actually had a good time.

After the party, Emmy had driven him home, helped him

take Seamus out for a walk, and then gotten his staggering ass back up to his apartment.

"Whoa," Padraig said, bumping his arm on the doorframe as Emmy led Seamus inside and took off his leash. The walk in the cool night air had helped sober him up a little bit. Mercifully. Then he realized he didn't know how he'd gotten from the Collins Dorm to here. Or how the party had ended. Had it ended?

"Shit. Blackout."

"I know, but the power's back on now," Emmy said.

"No. I think I blacked out." He'd made the mistake of shaking his head as he spoke, the action making him dizzy.

She studied with an amused grin. "You okay there, big guy?"

"Yeah, but is the room swaying? Feels like we're on a boat."

Emmy reached out to take his hand, pulling him into his wobbly apartment. "Apartment is holding steady. You? Not so much."

He closed the door behind him, throwing the lock. Leaning against it for support, he answered Emmy's questioning gaze. "You're not walking home alone. It's dark as sin out there tonight."

She glanced around. "I'll sleep on the couch. Not sure I should leave you alone like this anyway."

He shook his head. "Not couch. You can...have...my...bed..." As he spoke, he slowly slid down the door until he was sitting on the floor. He looked around. "I'll sleep here."

She laughed and reached down to him. "Nope. You're sleeping in your own bed. It's closer to the bathroom, which might be something you need later."

He accepted her proffered hands, but rather than letting her pull him up, he tugged her down until she was sitting on the floor next to him. "It's comfy down here, right? You're a sexy strawberry."

Emmy rolled her eyes. "And you're a sweet, if sloppy, drunk farmer."

Seamus came over, clearly confused but delighted to have them on his level for once. He licked Emmy's face affectionately as she giggled.

"He loves you," Padraig mused. "He loved Mia too." The words came easily, without the typical flash of pain, which told Padraig exactly how wasted he was.

"Come on, Farmer Collins. Let's pour you into bed."

This time, he let her drag him to his feet. Wrapping an arm around his waist, she steadied him as they walked down the hall to his bedroom. Once there, he sank down on the edge of the mattress and fought with the buttons on his flannel shirt.

The blackout had ended a little while earlier, but neither of them sought to turn on any lights. He lived on a city street, so the street-lamps outside provided just enough light for them to see each other and the room through the gray dimness.

Emmy smacked his fingers away and efficiently unbuttoned his shirt. He shrugged it off, then pointed to his dresser. "Second drawer down," he directed. "T-shirt." She opened it, grabbed one, and held it out to him.

He shook his head as he gripped her hips and turned her away from him. Sliding down the zipper at the back of her dress, he said, "For you. Dress is pretty but not to sleep in."

"Thanks," she said softly. "I'm going to run to the bathroom to put it on. Don't pass out yet."

He remained on the side of his bed, struggling to sit still, and he realized Emmy was right. The swaying was coming from him.

Shit. Or maybe not. Now the room was spinning. That wasn't good.

He fought with his boots, letting out a small cheer for himself when he finally managed to kick them off.

Emmy was only gone a moment or two. When she returned, she was wearing his T-shirt, the soft cotton hanging to just above her knees.

He chuckled. "The shirt is as long as your dress."

"You're a big guy," she pointed out.

"Naw. You're tiny. Naught but a wee fairy," he said with an Irish accent, "as my Pop Pop would say."

"Here." Emmy handed him three Advil and a cup of water. "This might help stave off some of tomorrow's hangover."

He took the pills and chugged the water. Placing the cup on the nightstand, he rose on unsteady legs and started to strip off his jeans.

Emmy took a step away. "I'll just grab a blanket and—"

"No. Wait." He reached out and grasped her wrist for just a second, making sure she stayed put. Then he shed his jeans, leaving his boxers on, as Emmy—the adorable woman—tried to look anywhere but at him.

Padraig pulled down the comforter and climbed into bed, his gaze landing on the empty side next to him. "Would you...can you sleep in here with me? Just until I pass out," he added quickly, when it was clear she planned to say no. "I'm tired of sleeping by myself."

"Seamus is already in there," she said, her tone laced with humor as they both looked at his mutt, sprawled out on his back at the foot of the bed, snoring.

"You know what I mean," he said.

Emmy considered his request for a moment, then crossed to the other side. "Okay. Just until you pass out."

She lay down next to him—on top of the covers—and he turned to look at her, his eyes suddenly heavy.

"Thanks for taking care of me tonight," he murmured, his voice low, the words somewhat slurred.

"That's what friends do," she whispered.

"Friends," he repeated, thinking she'd used the wrong word but too drunk to figure out the right one. Of course, he didn't have too long to ponder it before sleep claimed him.

. . .

THE NEXT MORNING, HE'D WOKEN UP IN BED ALONE, EMMY sacked out on his couch. While he'd felt like shit that next day, the darkness that had been swirling inside him had lifted and remained at bay.

Padraig tried once again to swallow down the tears, rubbing his eyes roughly, refusing to let them fall.

Then he recalled the remainder of the holidays that year. Eating a huge turkey dinner at Friendsgiving, and again on Thanksgiving, with Emmy by his side, both of them groaning in agony due to overeating. Emmy celebrating Christmas with his entire family for the first time, him cracking up at her overwhelmed, wide-eyed expression as she took it all in. He and Emmy hugging in the pub when the ball dropped on the New Year. Him giving her Conversation Hearts for Valentine's Day, joking that she could use the mushy-gushy lines in her next romance novel. Her stepping behind the bar on St. Patrick's Day to help him and his dad by working the taps until the crush of partiers thinned out.

She'd found a way to keep the darkness away. Simply by being there.

Cervical cancer.

The words rushed back in, accompanied by a wave of nausea.

"Fuck," he said. Then louder, "Fuck!"

Lifting his head, his gaze landed on the photograph of him and Mia on their wedding day. And the dam broke.

❧ 12 ❧

Padraig lay on his couch, not bothering to watch the highlights of a hockey game he had on mute. Instead, his gaze rested solely on the picture of him and Mia on their wedding day. Today was the third anniversary of Mia's death. It had been the first thing he'd thought of when he woke up this morning.

In truth, the date had been looming in the back of his mind for the past week or so. Part of him wondered if that knowledge had influenced his reaction to Emmy's test results. God knew that ever since he'd essentially lost his shit and walked away from her, he'd struggled to separate the sudden deluge of guilt he felt.

Guilt over moving on when Mia didn't have that chance.

Guilt over hurting Emmy so badly.

He couldn't stop seeing Mia's smile that last night just before she died or Emmy's eyes Thursday night when he'd broken her heart.

It had been three days since he'd walked away from her,

telling her he needed time. Both of them had read those words for the lie they were.

He'd known when he walked into her apartment, it was over. That he couldn't keep dating her, not if there was even a slim chance that he might lose her. But, like a coward, he'd avoided saying those words.

No. Avoided was the wrong word.

He hadn't been *able* to say them. They'd gotten lodged in his throat, strangling him until all he could do was turn tail and run, dropping that bullshit "I need time" line on her.

He'd spent Thursday night on the floor in front of the door in wet clothing, Seamus curled up next to him. He'd paid for that, waking up the next day with a stiff neck and the mother of all head colds. Since then, he'd called in sick to work, alternating his naps between his bed and the couch, lacking the energy, strength, or desire to do anything else.

Riley had shown up Friday, armed with chicken noodle soup, and his mother had come by yesterday with a plate of leftover roast from the Saturday dinner he'd missed. That was all he'd eaten in the last three days, and he wouldn't have consumed more than a few bites of either of the meals if his aunt and mother hadn't planted themselves next to him, waiting until he finished every bit.

Today, while he felt better physically, the bottom had dropped out on him emotionally.

There was no doubt his entire family knew what had happened between him and Emmy. Secrets didn't exist in the Collins clan.

Riley had asked where Emmy was and he'd choked on the words, simply shaking his head, only managing to say she wasn't there. He'd been too sick to shield his emotions, to hide the fact that he was down and out due to more than just a head cold. His aunt was too astute, too observant. She had inherited Pop Pop's sixth sense when it came to knowing things.

He suspected one phone call from Riley to Sunnie, followed by one call from Sunnie to Emmy, was all it would have taken for them to put the pieces together, to discover that he'd broken things off and why.

When his mom had shown up Saturday, he'd expected a third degree. He must have looked worse than he'd realized because she'd given him a bye, not mentioning Emmy's name at all. Which was good. Because he hadn't cried in front of his mother since he was a kid. He hadn't even let her see him fall apart after Mia's death because she'd been devastated by the loss as well.

But he was damn sure he wouldn't have been able to hold back the tears if she'd asked him about Emmy on Saturday, his emotions a train wreck, riding too close to the surface.

He closed his eyes wearily and sighed when he heard a knock on the door. He wasn't surprised someone was there. He was just curious who the family had elected as their spokesperson today.

Rising, he opened the door and spotted his first guess for today's visitor.

Pop Pop gave him an easy smile and held up a doggie bag from the pub. "Thought I'd see if you had your appetite back yet. Brought you your favorite comfort food."

"Burger and fries?"

Pop Pop nodded and handed him the bag, which Padraig took with a quick word of thanks.

Rather than open the food, he placed the bag on the coffee table and gestured toward a chair, silently inviting his grandfather to sit down.

"You feeling better?"

Padraig nodded. "Yeah. I can breathe again and my cough

is almost gone. I'll start back to work tomorrow," he said, even though he wasn't sure he would follow through on that. Being around people was the last thing he wanted at the moment. In fact, he'd prefer to hibernate right here in his apartment for the next decade or so, but there was no way in hell that was happening. If he didn't show up to work within the next day or two, a Collins mob would descend to drag him out.

"Good, good. Glad you're better," Pop Pop murmured. "I'm sure everyone will be happy to hear that. Your mom and aunts are worried."

"They don't need to be. I'm fine."

The look Pop Pop gave him told Padraig he didn't believe that lie for a second. "Health-wise, I suspect you *are* fine. But we both know there are different types of ailments." Pop Pop paused for just a moment before adding, "I know what day it is, Paddy. I just wanted to say that I miss that lovely girl too."

Padraig swallowed heavily. Pop Pop had been one of his main sources of support—along with Colm and Kelli—after Mia's passing. They'd both shared a similar grief, losing their wives far too early.

"Three years," Pop Pop mused.

Padraig nodded. "A long time."

Pop Pop shrugged. "Time is relative."

Padraig didn't know how to respond to that, so he didn't.

Pop Pop absentmindedly rubbed his knuckles. He suffered from arthritis, the result of a lifetime spent working with his hands. "I spoke to Kelli this morning. Apparently she and the girls went over to Emmy's last night, armed with margaritas."

Padraig gave his grandfather a ghost of a smile. "I'm glad they were there for her. I—" Padraig's throat closed painfully. She would need friends, since he couldn't be there for her himself. Even though it felt as if he'd ripped his own heart out, he knew that breaking things off was for the best. Walking away before...before things got too serious was better. For both of them. "I fucked up. Hurt her. Broke things off badly."

Pop Pop sighed. "I heard. Paddy..." he started.

Padraig waved his grandfather's words away. "I know what you're going to say, Pop Pop, but it's not going to change anything."

"What do you think I'm going to say?"

"That I overreacted." Padraig knew he had. He'd seen those test results and lost his shit. He should have taken some time, calmed down, approached Emmy with a more level head. Maybe then he wouldn't still ache over the pain he'd caused her.

"I don't think you overreacted, lad. I think you reacted the way anyone would when faced with their greatest fear."

"My greatest fear," Padraig repeated as he considered something he hadn't before, something he wanted his grandfather to confirm. "What's my greatest fear?"

"Losing someone you love."

"I don't think..." Padraig started, wanting to deny it but knowing he couldn't. "I *did* overreact. But I wasn't wrong. I can't do it again, Pop Pop. Can't feel that pain."

"And that's why you reacted the way you did. But, my dear lad, that's not a choice you can make, not something you can control."

"Actually it is. It's why I walked away," Padraig insisted, wondering if Pop Pop realized he was helping him make his case. "You have to see that. Have to understand that, right? I walked away before either of us could get hurt."

"Oh, I think it's safe to say that ship has sailed." Pop Pop leaned forward, resting his elbows on his knees. "Emmy makes you happy. That girl loves you. She'd give you the world if you'd accept it. But you're throwing that away because you're afraid. You can't let your fears rule you."

Padraig refused to listen. "When I saw that letter from Emmy's doctor, it brought up *everything*. Everything Mia went through. All the pain she suffered, that she'd been forced to endure. It wasn't fair to her. None of it was fair."

"You went through all that too, Padraig."

Padraig shook his head, but Pop Pop forged on, refusing to accept his denial. "You suffered too," his grandfather said insistently.

"You don't understand," Padraig argued, running a hand through his hair, certain it was standing on end after too many days lying in bed.

Pop Pop rubbed his jaw, a sadness in his eyes that Padraig didn't see too often. His grandfather was good at masking his darker feelings, never letting those he loved know he was sad or upset. Padraig had watched him shutter away his desolation over the fire at the pub countless times during their trip to Ireland.

"Of course I understand. Better than perhaps anyone. It wasn't easy for me to watch Sunday suffer all those months. To see the cancer slowly eating away at her, consuming her until there was nothing left. The love of my life was dying by inches, and there wasn't a damn thing I could do to save her. That sort of helplessness leaves a deep, deep scar."

"If you know that, then why..." Padraig wasn't sure how to word his question.

"Why am I asking you to risk that pain again?"

Padraig nodded.

"Because you're young, and there's a beautiful, sweet woman just a few blocks away who's offering you a second chance at true happiness. There are a great many things you didn't have the opportunity to experience with Mia. Fatherhood, buying a house, raising a family, bickering over money, fighting over what to name your fourth son because you'd already used all the boy names you could agree on. I had all of that. Sunday and I had decades together; you and Mia had but one year."

"I get that, but..." He paused. Padraig wouldn't waste the breath to lie to his grandfather, to say he didn't want to be a father someday. That feeling had always been there, but he'd buried it deep after Mia's death, fighting hard to snuff it out, to douse that fire by denying it kindling. However, it wouldn't flicker out, and lately, every time he saw Colm with the twins or Fergus texted a picture of Sophie, it sparked bright again.

"Things were different for me, Paddy. I had a houseful of children—seven devastated kids—all looking to me to care for them. I couldn't—wouldn't—divide my attention, my time. They'd already lost so much. Too much. So I wrapped my life around them because I believed that was what they needed. But now..."

"But now?" Padraig prompted.

"But now...I'm not so sure it was what *I* needed. The real reason I'm telling you to overcome your fear is because..." Pop Pop took a deep breath. "I know all the ways to the depths of my soul that you are a stronger man than I."

Padraig didn't have a clue how to respond to that. His grandfather was one of the strongest men he knew. "That's not true."

"It is."

"What are you saying?"

"I'm asking you, Paddy, to have the courage I didn't. I'm an old man, and I've had a lot of time to look back on my life, to reflect on the decisions I've made. There are things I regret. Sometimes I wonder if I'd opened my eyes and looked around, if I'd risked my heart again, if I would have found an Emmy, a second chance at love and happiness."

Padraig had never—not once—heard Pop Pop talk about finding someone else. He'd always claimed he'd met and married his soul mate, that Sunday had been it for him forever. "I didn't know you felt that way."

"Look at how long I've lived without Sunday. Another whole lifetime. If I'd taken the chance I'm telling you to take right now, I might have lived the second half of my life with a woman I could have loved every bit as much as Sunday. As I said before, time is relative. But maybe more importantly, love isn't finite."

"You still miss Grandma Sunday. You still love her."

"I do. Just as you're always going to miss and love Mia. But you're far too young to doom yourself to a life alone."

Padraig nodded, Pop Pop's words sinking in deep as the guilt that had been sucking him down like quicksand suddenly loosened, his grandfather throwing him a rope, allowing him a chance to climb out. What would he give to live as a free man?

He saw Emmy's face again in his mind. He'd walked away because of fear and the end result was the same. He'd still lost her, and the pain of that was unbearable.

Pop Pop looked down, studying the floor for a few moments before he lifted his gaze to him and continued speaking. "I'm a man like any other, lad. And going to bed night after night, year after year, is lonely. I wouldn't wish it on anyone, and I definitely don't wish it for you. Give your heart to Emmy. She's perfect for you. She adores you, and I don't doubt for a moment she will fill your days and nights with laughter and love and a houseful of kids if you want. Don't throw all of that away because of fear. Do you love Emmy?"

"Yes. God, yes," he replied without a second's hesitation.

"Then that means taking a risk. Neither of you can give the other any guarantees. That's not how life works. Nothing is certain. But love...well, that's the only thing that makes life worth living, that gives us a reason to get up every morning."

Padraig considered those words, and once again, he recalled Emmy's face on Thursday night. "I hurt her."

Pop Pop nodded. "So make it right."

"I don't know if I can. I walked away from her when she needed me. My behavior...it was unforgiveable."

"I don't believe that. You're human. You made an understandable mistake when faced with a genuine fear. One you now recognize and can fight against in the future."

"What if I've already lost her?" Now that Pop Pop had shone a light on what his future could hold, Padraig wanted it with all his heart.

"You didn't. You just need to convince Emmy you're not merely talking the talk. You have to walk the walk."

Padraig chuckled. "You sound like Kelli there."

Pop Pop grinned. "That's exactly who I'm quoting. She came by the pub this morning full of piss and vinegar, prepared to, and I quote, 'kick his ass and drag him kicking and screaming if I have to' back to Emmy, to make things right. Your father and I convinced her I might be a more levelheaded spokesperson."

"Walk the walk, huh?"

"Which means taking your time. Having patience. You can't look at this relationship with Emmy through the Mia lens."

"Time is relative," Padraig repeated, suddenly understanding. "I get it. I can do that. I *will* do that."

"I believe in you, Paddy. You can do anything you put your mind to. Apologize—grovel, if necessary—but make it right.

Then grab that girl with both hands and hold on tight. I promise, if you do that, you'll be able to live your life without regrets."

"Okay. Yeah," he said, smiling for the first time in days.

"Good." Pop Pop rose as Padraig walked him to the door. His grandfather reached out and gave him a warm hug. "Make me proud, lad. I love you," he said as he left.

Padraig returned to the couch, feeling a thousand pounds lighter than he had just an hour earlier. His stomach growled, and he grinned, reaching for the burger and fries.

Between the food and Pop Pop's visit, Padraig felt ready to take on the world, ready to claim the woman he loved.

But first...there was someone else he needed to talk to.

An hour later, Padraig stood before Mia's tombstone, a bouquet of flowers in his hands. The sky was overcast, the gloomy, gray weather holding on tight after the storms from a few nights earlier.

"Hey, you," he said softly, placing the flowers on the grass in front of her grave. He knelt down, running his finger over Mia's name carved in the stone, then along the month and day—today's date. "It's been three years, Mia. I miss you so much."

He glanced around at the sound of leaves crunching and grinned at Seamus, whom he'd tied to a nearby tree. The dog's tail was waving enthusiastically, rustling a pile of dry leaves, as a squirrel scampered by. He and Seamus visited Mia's grave together several times a year, on her birthday, which was also their wedding anniversary, the anniversary of the day they met, and today.

He always brought flowers and he always talked to her. It was Pop Pop who'd encouraged him to speak to Mia during his visits, confiding he'd been conversing with Sunday for decades about the kids and grandkids and life in general.

Padraig had felt silly the first time because he knew she wasn't really there, but...well...maybe he had too much of Pop Pop's belief in Irish magic flowing through his veins because he never failed to feel her presence.

"I've met someone," he said. "Her name is Emmy. She's a romance writer."

Padraig chuckled, recalling Mia's love of soap operas. "You'd love her books. And her. Seamus is crazy about her. She's so sweet, Mia. She's become a good friend the past couple of years. She's been there for me, helped me get through the times when I was missing you so bad, I physically ached with it."

He dropped from his knees to his ass, sitting in front of her tombstone. If he closed his eyes, he could almost imagine the two of them sitting across the kitchen table from each other. Mia had always been easy to talk to. It was one of the many things she and Emmy had in common.

"I'm in love with her, Mia," he confessed. "I didn't know... I wasn't sure I could fall in love after you. Colm always talks about the Collins curse, about how members of my family fall fast and forever. It certainly happened that way for you and me. And I'm going to love you forever. I don't want you to think that's changed. It's just...I love her too. Cursed twice," he said with a chuckle. "Normal people might think that sounds unlucky, but I feel like the luckiest man alive. To have had you in my life. And now her. I think you'd understand that."

A breeze rustled the leaves and one took flight, landing right on his lap. He smiled at her name, engraved in the granite. "Yeah. I knew you would."

Colm would give him shit for thinking the leaf a sign, but

Pop Pop would agree wholeheartedly that he was interpreting the leaf as Mia's response correctly.

When the gray clouds held back the rain he'd thought imminent when he'd first arrived, he sighed contentedly and settled in for a longer visit, telling her about the pub rebuild, Fergus's new baby, and all the family gossip.

An hour later, he rose to leave.

"I'm going to go for now, Mia. I'll be back soon, promise."

He'd just unhooked Seamus from the tree when the clouds broke and the first ray of sunshine Baltimore had seen in days broke through.

Bright and yellow and...happy.

He gazed heavenward, then smiled back at Mia's grave.

"I love you too," he whispered.

❄ 13 ❄

Padraig walked into the pub, aware he was late. It was his first day back at work since walking away from Emmy on Thursday. Uncle Ewan had called him yesterday to say they were going to start holding Monday morning meetings—as part of his grand scheme to increase business at both the pub and the restaurant.

While Padraig and his dad had spent the time after the fire touring Ireland, Ewan had put that time away from work to even better use, capitalizing on improvements, researching marketing, and throwing a serious amount of energy behind creating special events, like the upcoming blowout he had planned for St. Patrick's Day in two days' time.

Padraig hung his jacket behind the counter, then followed the sound of voices over to Sunday's Side, shocked to discover this meeting was a bit bigger than he'd expected. He'd anticipated it would be him, Dad, Riley, Keira, and Ewan. To his surprise, Killian, Sean, and Teagan were also in attendance. It was rare to see all seven of the Collins siblings together in one place, with the exception of holidays and weddings.

"What's going on?" he asked.

They'd pushed two tables together in the restaurant, the top of them covered with cups of coffee and a large platter of doughnuts.

Dad glanced up, a Boston Crème halfway to his lips, and said, "You're late."

"I'm aware. Where's Yvonne?" Padraig asked. She appeared to be the only person missing from this powwow.

"Reba had a fever last night. She's taking her to the doctor this morning. Thinks it might be an ear infection," Ewan replied.

Keira stood up and placed her hand against his forehead, in true concerned aunt form, uncaring that he was a thirty-four-year-old man. "How are you feeling? You still look a little pale."

"I'm fine, Aunt Keira."

Teagan eyeballed him as if unconvinced. "Your voice sounds hoarse. You sure you don't need another day of rest?"

"I'm good," he reassured his aunts, grinning at the way his uncles and father were rolling their eyes. All of the men in the family were used to being coddled by the females. Padraig figured it was a fair trade, considering the males were infamous for their overprotectiveness when it came to the women in their lives.

Tit for tat and all that.

"Good," Sean said. "Then sit down and grab a doughnut before your father eats them all."

"I've only had three," Dad said gruffly. "Riley made four dozen, for God's sake."

"Because I planned to take the leftovers to the precinct for Aaron and his men. But between you and Killian, I'll be lucky to have half a dozen left."

Killian gave her a wide smile as he popped the last bite of

a jelly-filled into his mouth. "I regret nothing," he said as he reached for another.

Riley rose from her seat farther down the table, reaching for the platter, intent on taking it away from them, but Sean pulled it out of her grasp before she could grab it, blowing his sister a playful kiss to show he'd won when he helped himself to a coconut doughnut.

Riley threw up her hands, then lunged quickly, managing to grab a glazed doughnut for herself. "The cops can fend for themselves," she joked, though there wasn't a person in the room who didn't know that merely meant she'd make another batch for them later.

Padraig had just reached for his own doughnut when Riley smacked his hand away. "Hey. I haven't even had one," he complained.

"And you're not going to until you tell me what I want to hear."

Padraig glanced around the table and realized there wasn't a person there who didn't know exactly what Riley was referring to. It warmed his heart to know they were all as crazy about Emmy as he was. "Pop Pop already talked to me yesterday."

"Mmm-hmmm," Riley said. "Him talking doesn't tell me a damn thing about you listening."

"Riley," Dad murmured. "Paddy doesn't need you interfering in his love life."

"I listened to him," Padraig reassured her.

"I'm glad," Teagan chimed in. "I would hate for you to let your fears stand in the way of your dreams. I almost lost Sky because I was too afraid to leave home, and look at the life I've led since then."

Padraig had heard Sky and Teagan's story many times before.

"Besides," Sean added, "there's nothing better than falling in love with your best friend." Something Sean would know, considering he'd fallen for both of his best friends, Lauren and Chad. "You and Emmy know each other well. That makes for a strong foundation."

Padraig nodded. "I'm crazy about her. But I've got a lot of making up to do. I really fucked up."

"There's nothing you can't fix," Ewan interjected.

"Pop Pop said the same thing."

Ewan wiped his sticky fingers on a napkin. "That's because it's true. Love isn't always easy, but it's always worth fighting for. I had to fight hard to win Natalie's heart. And damned if it wasn't worth it. Fight for Emmy."

Padraig recalled how he'd promised he would always fight for her the night he'd broken up her date with Joe.

He'd broken that promise...briefly. He wouldn't do so again.

Padraig appreciated everyone's pep talk, perfectly aware they were all speaking from experience. The people surrounding him had found and fought hard for their relationships.

After visiting Mia's grave, Padraig had returned home in the early evening, physically exhausted. While the worst of his cold had passed, the day's events had worn him out and he'd been dog-tired, so he decided he wanted one more night to fully recover before facing Emmy. Plus, he still wasn't sure what he could say to make things right...but he had some thoughts.

"I'm going to see her today. Right after work."

"Perfect." Riley lifted the tray of doughnuts. "You can have one now."

He laughed, and then the subject turned to planning the St. Patrick's Day event. It turned out Teagan was at the meeting because Ewan had shanghaied her into performing. Killian and Sean were there simply because they heard there would be doughnuts.

For the next two hours, they chiseled out all the details, and Padraig had to admit that even with so much still up in the air in terms of his future, he was excited for the holiday. And praying he could talk Emmy into being there.

"Okay—time to get ready to open up for lunch," Riley said, even though she'd been bouncing back and forth between the kitchen and the meeting the entire time, checking on her specials, taking her baked goods out of the oven.

They all rose, but no one seemed in a hurry to leave. Padraig left his dad chatting with his siblings while he went over to get things rolling on the pub side. At ten thirty, he unlocked the door and returned to his station behind the bar. Squatting down, he checked the connections on the taps.

He heard the bell jingle, announcing someone's arrival. Rising, he was about to tell whoever it was to grab a seat anywhere...when he saw Emmy, hovering in the doorway.

She obviously hadn't seen him, stooped down as he was, so her eyes widened when he rose.

She hesitated.

"You coming in?" he asked, giving her a friendly smile, recalling he'd asked her the same question the very first day she'd come to the pub.

"Yeah." Approaching the bar, she stopped next to her usual stool but didn't sit down. "I heard you were sick. Are you feeling better?"

He was touched by her concern. "I am." Then he added, "Kelli texted me this morning. She said you got the results of your second pap smear and it's all good."

She nodded. "It is. I know you asked for some time, Paddy, but I—"

"Em. About that," he interjected.

"No, please," she said. "Just hear me out."

He fell silent. The least he could do was give her a chance to speak her piece. She deserved to rail at him, cuss him out, give him hell. Part of him hoped she would, simply to help him assuage some of the guilt he felt. He would take whatever she dished out as his due for his horrible behavior.

"I've been thinking about what happened...and I don't think just taking some time apart will fix it."

"I shouldn't have behaved that way, shouldn't have left the way I did. I'm so sorry, Emmy," Padraig said, reaching out to place his hand on hers where it rested on the bar.

Emmy pulled it away before he could touch her. He lowered his hand, resting it on the counter.

She was avoiding his touch. And his gaze. Regardless, he could tell she planned to do what he couldn't on Thursday.

Break things off.

Little did she know, things had changed. He'd fight for her until his last dying breath.

Emmy Martin was his, from now until forever, and he'd do whatever it took to prove his love to her.

Emmy folded her hands in front of her, hiding them behind the bar so that Padraig wouldn't see they were trembling. The night he left, she'd fallen into her bed, crying inconsolably, hoping against hope that he'd come to his senses, that he'd come back to her.

However, by the time morning came, her tears had evaporated. Because as much as it killed her, she understood. All the way to the depths of her soul. She understood why he'd walked away.

Her girlfriends had shown up last night, armed with margaritas, expecting she would need their help to find her footing. Emmy could tell they'd been surprised to discover she wasn't in a fetal position in the corner. They'd anticipated needing to bolster her spirits, to dry her tears.

Instead, they found her calm, resigned.

So rather than trying to cheer her up, they'd switched gears, insisting Padraig would come to his senses.

Emmy held no such hope. She had spent the last two years of her life clinging to the hope that he could care for her, that he could love her as much as he did Mia.

What she hadn't considered, hadn't realized, was just how deep his suffering went. His actions in any relationship from now on would always be influenced by Mia, and that was something Emmy simply couldn't live with.

So she was cutting her losses. Moving on.

She cleared the lump forming in her throat, determined to say what she'd come to say and leave. If she was lucky, she'd be able to get through this without falling completely apart. "You said you needed time to think. Turns out, I did too."

He held her gaze, his expression unreadable, so she forged on.

"Here's the thing, Paddy. I can't promise I'm never going to get a sniffle, never going to get sick or injured. And I definitely can't promise to outlive you. Those are reassurances you seem to need that I can never provide."

Padraig shook his head. "Jesus, Em. I don't need that."

She refused to back down. "You thought you were ready, I get that. But you aren't, and I can't keep waiting, can't keep hoping for something you may never be able to give me."

Padraig raised his hand to stop her. "I am ready, Em."

She shook her head. "No. You aren't." She couldn't spend another night like last Thursday. Couldn't wait around for the next bad or scary news that sent him running.

"Please give me another chance, let me make this right." Padraig's jaw was tight, and she allowed herself to look at him —*really* look at him. He had dark shadows under his eyes, stress lines around his mouth, several days' extra growth on his jaw that indicated he either hadn't had the energy to shave or he was growing back the beard he'd sported when they'd first met.

She took a deep breath and forced herself to say the most important thing that had sent her here this morning. "I can't live in Mia's shadow."

Padraig froze for a moment, just long enough to convince her she'd hit the nail on the head. "Her shadow?"

The confusion in his voice was her undoing, the last of her energy zapped. She had to get out of here.

"Goodbye," she whispered, turning quickly.

She'd almost made it to the door when Padraig caught up to her, grasping her upper arm to halt her escape. She whirled around, digging deep for the strength that would give her the ability to end this once and for all.

Her gaze narrowed on his hand on her arm. "Padraig."

He released her arm but only so that he could step closer, cup her face in his large, calloused palms. "Emmy."

She tried to shrug out of his grip, but he refused to let her escape.

She stilled completely when he said, "You aren't in Mia's shadow. You've *never* been there."

She started to shake her head, but he tightened his hold.

"Listen to me. I need you to understand this. When I met Mia, she lit up a place inside me that I didn't know existed. She taught me what love was, how precious life is. When she died, that light went out and the world was dark—pitch black —for too long."

He leaned closer, the heat of his breath on her face as he continued, "Then I met you. You're different from her. You aren't a light, Emmy."

"What?" she asked, her voice breaking.

"And you aren't standing in any shadow." She frowned until he added, "You can't be, because you're the whole goddamn sun."

Emmy stared at him, stunned. "I'm the sun?"

He nodded, then took advantage of her shock by bending forward and kissing her. It was a soft kiss, an apology and a promise rolled up in one. "You found me at my darkest point. You saved me, then you reminded me of all those lessons Mia taught me. I'm so in love with you, Emmy, I can't see straight. You're everything to me. God, you're *everything*."

Emmy let his words wash through her as she searched for a reply. For once, words failed her, deserted her completely.

It didn't matter because Padraig wasn't giving her a chance to speak. He kissed her again, this one harder, longer, pure passion. He retained his grip on her face, refusing to release her lips. Not that she was trying to back away. She'd breathe again tomorrow. For now, all she wanted was him. This kiss.

This moment to last forever.

She was the sun.

When they parted, she smiled. "I love you too."

Padraig's entire face lit up. "I'm never walking away from you again," he vowed. "I know I hurt you, know my actions were unforgiveable—"

"Paddy, I understand why you—"

"Understand or not, I was wrong and I know it."

"It doesn't matter now...because I'm never going to let you do that again," she said, needing him to know that while she understood, she couldn't watch him walk away from her again. "I'll bar the door, tie you to the bed, kick your ass. You're mine, and I'm not letting you go."

He chuckled. "My kinky girl." Then his face sobered. "Always fighting for me. I'm not going anywhere. I swear it." He glanced over his shoulder toward the bar as if he'd just recalled something. "Don't move." He took a step away from her. "I have a present for you. I was going to bring it by your place after work."

"I don't need a present."

Padraig ignored her as he quickly stepped behind the bar and pulled a small wrapped box out of his coat pocket before returning to her. "Here."

She unwrapped it, and when she pulled the lid off, her eyes widened. "Paddy," she breathed.

"It's a rock."

Emmy laughed. "I can see that."

"It has a story."

She gave him a playful look that said *duh*. "Of course it does. All rocks have stories."

"This one has a very special story." Padraig reached in and pulled the rock out, holding it on his palm so she could look at it more closely. "I found this rock behind the pub, the morning after the fire."

"You did?"

He nodded. "I have no idea why I picked it up, but when I did, it was still warm from the heat of the blaze."

Emmy studied the charred rock, understanding now why parts of it were black.

"I tucked it in the inside pocket of my coat for some reason and forgot about it. I didn't realize it was still there until I found it again last week. That was when it told me its story, told me it was *your* rock."

"Mine? Why?" she asked.

"As you can see, it's suffered quite a lot. Endured a great deal of pain. This rock had to stand witness as its home burned down around it. It watched as its whole world was reduced to ash."

Emmy looked at the black scorch marks, aware that Padraig wasn't just telling the rock's story.

"But these scorch marks only tell a small part of the tale, because if you flip it over..." Padraig lifted his hand toward her, prompting her to turn the rock over, so she did. "The original rock still remains. It was always there. Just hidden underneath the charring. The rock said it needs a special owner—you—because you're the only one who can see what's still there, buried beneath the pain. You're the one who will always make sure that it lives in the sunshine, that it doesn't get lost in the darkness, in the soot and ashes again."

Emmy ran her finger over the smooth surface of the rock. "You're right," she whispered. "It *is* a very special rock." She took it from his hand, closing it tightly in her palm. "I'll always take care of it."

He kissed her cheek. "I know you will. And maybe someday, you'll tell our kids that rock's story, along with all the others."

Our kids.

Two words had never sounded so beautiful.

"I will," she promised, her heart nearly bursting with happiness at the genuine joy on his face.

"And one day—when you're ready, because I don't want to rush this—I plan on giving you a different kind of rock. One I hope you'll wear on this finger," he said, pointing to the fourth finger on her left hand, "for the rest of your life."

"I like the sound of that," she confessed.

"Good." Padraig lowered his head and kissed her again as

she wrapped her arms around his shoulders, feeling that after a lifetime of searching and hoping, she'd finally found her hero, her alpha male, her happily ever after.

The two of them parted, smiling at each other.

"Can we come out and hug you both yet?"

Emmy turned at the sound of Riley's voice coming from Sunday's Side and laughed when she spied not just Padraig's aunt but his father and a couple uncles standing in the opening between the restaurant and the pub.

"Were you eavesdropping on all of that?" Padraig asked exasperatedly.

"Not exactly," Riley replied as she and—to Emmy's shock —the rest of the Collins siblings walked over to them.

All seven of them were there. Even Teagan.

"Did you sell tickets?" Emmy teased Padraig, who was shaking his head, though she wasn't sure if he was amused or resigned by his family's appearance.

"Nosy bastards," he muttered. "What does 'not exactly' mean, Riley?"

"It means we couldn't hear a damn word you were saying," Tris admitted. "You weren't talking loud enough. Something you need to work on. So we had to make due with Riley's play-by-play as she kept sneaking peeks through the opening. Thought Ewan and I were going to have to run interference and cut Emmy off at the pass when she started to leave."

Emmy was touched that they would go to such lengths to help her and Padraig get back together. "That's sweet," she said, giving Tris a kiss on the cheek.

"I thought my boy got some of that sweetness from me," Tris told her with a wink before looking at Padraig. "But we're going to have to talk about your gift-giving skills, son, because a rock is a strange way to win a woman's heart."

Emmy laughed. "It's the perfect gift. I love it."

"Which proves that you've found the right woman for you," Ewan said, slapping Padraig on the shoulder. "Don't fuck it up."

He gave his uncle a mock salute. "Duly noted."

"You kids get out of here," Tris said. "I'll cover your shift today."

Padraig clearly didn't need to be asked twice as he reached for Emmy's hand. "Your place or mine," he asked, when they reached the sidewalk outside.

"Our place," she replied.

Padraig frowned, confused. "Which is?"

"Whichever one we choose. Think you can borrow some of those moving boxes from Oliver?"

Padraig smiled, tugging her close enough to kiss the side of her head. "Damn, woman. Slow down. You're always in such a hurry to get to the next part. You *really* need to stop and smell the roses."

❧ 14 ❧

They walked into Padraig's apartment hand in hand, Seamus jumping excitedly when he saw Emmy.

"Down," Padraig commanded, the dog listening for all of three seconds before jumping up again in an attempt to lick Emmy's face.

Emmy didn't mind, laughing as she rubbed Seamus's head and told the dog how much she'd missed him.

"Starting to wonder if you're here for me or Seamus," Padraig teased.

Emmy gave him a mischievous grin over her shoulder. "You'll never know."

Padraig laughed as he twisted her body away from his dog to press her against the closed door. He kissed her once more because he simply couldn't wait another second. After spending the past few days genuinely believing he'd never be with her again, it felt as if he'd won the lottery after ten hungry years on the streets.

Emmy's kiss proved she felt the same.

"Never again," Padraig promised before resuming their kiss.

"Never again," she whispered, repeating the vow. "Whatever comes our way," she added, and Padraig realized she still needed his reassurance.

"I promise, Emmy." And as he said the words, he vowed he would indeed walk the walk. There was no other choice. Without her, life wasn't worth living. "Want to move this party to the bedroom?"

She laughed breathlessly and nodded.

Padraig clasped her hand in his and started to lead her down the hall, but he was pulled up short as Emmy dug in her heels.

"Paddy," she gasped.

He grinned, fully aware of what had captured her attention. She had spotted a new photo on his wall, one she hadn't seen before. It was of the two of them on Halloween, the night of the blackout, the night she'd taken care of him.

He'd asked his dad to snap the picture of them in their farmer and strawberry costumes in the pub, just before heading to the party upstairs. Emmy was cheesing for the camera while Padraig was looking at her. Dad had texted the photo to him that night, and Padraig had saved it, looking at it more times than he cared to admit over the last year or so.

Last night, he'd sat down on his couch, scrolling through the pictures on his phone as he mulled over how to mend things with her. The more he looked, the more he realized the majority of the photos on his phone were of Emmy—the two of them together in some, or her with Seamus, or just her alone—and he was reminded once again of exactly how important, how vital, she'd become to his happiness, offering him true friendship, and now...love.

"I can't believe you framed this and hung it up."

"Why wouldn't I?" he asked, watching as Emmy's eyes traveled to the other framed pictures.

"Oh!" she said. "You hung all of them up."

He'd replaced all but one of the photos of Mia, keeping the one of them on their wedding day.

In the others' places now, there was a photo of Seamus, one of Colm and Kelli with the twins, and the great one of him and Pop Pop chatting together while at the pub that Emmy had given him for Christmas this year. She'd actually gifted him most of the pictures, but he'd never hung them up, refusing to relinquish a single spot in what he now knew had become a shrine to Mia, another way he'd locked himself in the past, in his grief.

"It reminds me of Pop Pop's wall now," he said. "Filled with the faces of everyone I love."

She smiled and kissed him on the cheek. "I love it. Love that I snagged a spot."

He smiled back. "You snagged a spot here too," he said, pointing to his heart. "And you're about to snag one down there." Padraig pointed down the hall to his bedroom. He turned her away from him, swatting her on the ass. "If you'd hurry up and get a move on."

Emmy didn't start walking. "You're not giving me much incentive." As she spoke, she wiggled her adorable ass at him, inviting him to spank her again.

Padraig laughed, then wrapped his arm around her shoulders, moving once more toward his bedroom.

When they reached it, he resumed their kiss, loving the way Emmy's hands caressed his cheeks, toyed with his short beard.

"Growing it back?" she asked.

He nodded. "Yeah. I think so. Like it?"

"I love it. Reminds me of the day we met. I took one look

at you and thought, 'It's about time you got here.' It felt as though I'd been meandering around aimlessly...looking for you."

"I took my wedding ring off that day. Right after you left."

"I didn't know that."

Padraig had never confessed that to her. He'd worn the ring over a year after Mia's death. Then he'd met Emmy and seen a kindred spirit. She'd been knocked down by her parents' deaths, but unlike him, she'd gotten back up, started putting one foot in front of the other, forced herself to move forward. "Your optimism, your desire to embrace life...it inspired me to do the same. Of course, it took me a lot longer to figure out how to do that. Thankfully, I've had one hell of an adorable tour guide."

"Just adorable?" she asked, her tone pure seductress.

"Sexy as sin."

She obviously liked that response. Emmy tugged at the hem of his shirt and he helped her, the two of them drawing it over his head together. Hers followed next.

Neither of them bothered with patience, both racing to strip the other of all their clothing. Once they were naked, Padraig pulled her into his arms again, his hands exploring every inch of her he could reach.

Then he pushed her toward the bed. She climbed into the middle and he followed Emmy down, caging her beneath him as they kissed, stroked, touched, driving each other higher and higher.

"I know I promised to help you fulfill that list of fantasies, but tonight...all I want to do is get lost in those pretty blue eyes of yours while I make love to you."

Emmy's legs parted. "That's the ultimate fantasy," she whispered.

He guided the head of his cock to her pussy, their gazes

locked together as he slowly slid inside. Once he was seated to the hilt, he kissed her again and again as he began to thrust.

Emmy lifted her legs, locking her ankles behind his back, tilting her hips so he could slip in even deeper.

Padraig moved faster, driving in harder as Emmy's fingernails scored his bare shoulders. Reaching down with one hand, he stroked her clit, loving the way she cried out with pleasure, her body jerking in response.

Emmy came loudly, his name on her lips. Padraig gave her the briefest of reprieves before moving once more, needing her like he needed oxygen. He would never get enough of her.

Emmy cupped his face, lifting her head from the pillow to steal more kisses.

"Love you," she murmured. "Love you so fucking much."

"Language," he teased. The two of them laughed even as he continued to thrust inside her, the sound cut short by his climax striking hard and fast.

This—this was what Emmy had brought back to his life.

Laughter. Friendship. Romance. Sunshine. Love.

A second wonderful, wild chance at happiness.

Two nights later, Padraig stood at the end of the bar, taking a breather for a moment and looking around the pub, which was busting at the seams with family and friends and regulars, all ready to celebrate St. Patrick's Day in style. The place was awash in green—thanks to Ewan's decorations, countless pitchers and pints of green beer, and everyone's attire.

If they'd held a contest for the best outfits, Ryder and Darcy would have won, the two of them sporting matching green T-shirts. Ryder's said, "We're pregnant, but mostly her," while Darcy's said, "You can stop asking me when we're having a baby now." Padraig had to admit his family always found clever, funny ways to announce they were expecting.

The family had gone mad when Darcy and Ryder had taken off their winter coats and started making their rounds of the room. Apparently, the pregnancy hadn't been planned and had taken them both by surprise, though no one could tell that from the delighted smiles on their faces.

Padraig had managed to slip away from his duties as bartender earlier for just a few minutes when he pulled Emmy to the dance floor, drawing her into his arms for a slow dance. Teagan had stopped by the bar at the beginning of her second set, proclaiming she was about to perform his and Emmy's song and she expected to see the two of them dancing. He'd told Teagan they didn't have a song, but she'd informed him that they did, and she was singing it, and he and Emmy were dancing to it.

When she said it in that stubborn Collins way, Padraig knew resistance was futile.

Teagan introduced a Kacey Musgraves song called "Rainbow," and Padraig had to admit his aunt had found them the perfect song. The lyrics felt like they'd been written just for him and Emmy.

He had been walking around like a man lost in a storm for so many years. Then Emmy came along and reminded him to look up. To see the rainbow over his head. After the song ended, he'd kissed Emmy, told her he loved her, and returned to his station behind the bar. From there, he watched as she walked over to the stage to thank Teagan.

He stretched briefly, silently hoping he found the opportunity to steal at least one more dance with Emmy before the night was over. Though he wasn't sure his chances were good. Ewan had organized one hell of a party.

He was about to return to his spot behind the bar when he heard Finn say, "He reached for a wipe!"

Padraig rolled his eyes, glancing toward the table most of his male cousins and brother had claimed. He laughed when he realized Lochlan and Finn were each making a case for their side of the wing argument to Colm. It appeared that once again, they were fighting over the last wing on the platter. Colm listened with great interest, asking questions to clarify the parts he was fuzzy on, then he told them they were both right—just before snagging the last wing, declaring it his retainer fee for taking the case.

The argument might have continued if Aunt Riley hadn't shown up at that point with a huge platter of potato skins.

"Should we hammer out the finer points of potato skins etiquette before we eat?" Oliver's suggestion probably would have held more weight if he'd said it before stuffing one into his mouth, a big glob of sour cream on his lower lip.

Emmy was currently in the middle of a huge circle of Collins women on the dance floor, she, Caitlyn, and Kelli skirting the line between tipsy and wasted, laughing and singing and shaking it like they'd just discovered music and dancing. Teagan, who was belting out one of her most popular songs, caught his eyes and tilted her head toward the girls and winked. He'd already made half a dozen pitchers of margaritas for the whole group of women and they were showing no signs of slowing down soon.

Ailis and Fiona were scream-singing near the stage, neither one too concerned with pitch or key. Padraig remembered Sky joking once that singing talent had skipped a generation with his and Teagan's daughters, teasingly telling them to "stop strangling the cat," which only ever encouraged Ailis and Fiona, the minxes, to sing louder and more off-key.

A loud cheer drew his attention to the back of the pub,

where they'd set up an area for darts. His uncles, Sean and Chad, had obviously just handed Justin and Killian their asses, their palms upward in the age-old "pay up" gesture. Killian pulled out his wallet but stopped when Justin loudly insisted on "double or nothing!" The chalkboard was quickly erased for round two despite the fact Hunter and Lucas complained that it was their turn to play the winners.

The Italian Stallions had claimed a large table in the middle of the pub with Aaron, Miguel, Landon, and a few of their cop friends. As always, the Moretti brothers drew a crowd, as no fewer than a dozen women hovered around, hoping to catch their eyes. Tony, the sexy bastard, had worn his hair down, much to every Collins woman's delight.

Padraig met Joe's gaze, the man lifting his mug and his eyebrows in a silent cheers. He nodded with a friendly grin, forced to admit Joe had definitely done him a solid when it came to Emmy, opening his eyes to what was standing right in front of him.

"Quite a night."

Padraig turned around and realized Pop Pop was doing the same survey of the room he was. "It really is."

"Quite a family," Pop Pop added.

Padraig grinned widely. "It really is," he repeated. "Of course, what do you expect? We're in a room full of young warriors and Vikings and kings."

"As well as beautiful, courageous ladies and saints and elf armies," Pop Pop added.

"And one peaceful dove, but let's don't bring that up in front of Colm. It's a bone of contention for him that his name doesn't mean something tough...or cool."

Pop Pop was clearly pleased Padraig recalled the meaning of everyone's names. The two of them continued to look around the room together, chuckling when they spotted Will and Keira sneaking off toward the storage closet like a couple of teenagers, hand in hand.

"Ewan's right. We need to put a lock on that closet to keep the family from using it as Lover's Lane," Padraig mused.

"No," Pop Pop said. "If we did that, it would only tie up the restrooms."

Padraig laughed. "Excellent point."

"Besides, Sunday and I availed ourselves of that storage closet on quite a few occasions as well. It was the only place we could sneak kisses without Sean or Riley catching us, proclaiming our show of affection 'gross.'"

"They seem to have changed their tunes on that," Padraig said as they watched Riley, who was delivering food, stopping behind Aaron to place an affectionate kiss on the top of his head. Aaron reached around, squeezing her butt as she swatted at him, laughing.

Another glance toward the darts game and Padraig spotted Sean and Chad high-fiving, just before giving each other a quick buss after hitting a bull's-eye.

"There's so much love in this room," Pop Pop said. Padraig followed his grandfather's gaze around the pub, taking it all in.

Pop Pop was right. Everywhere he looked, he saw it. He saw it in the way Sunnie and Darcy excitedly talked about babies, rubbing each other's stomachs, as Bubbles wiped away a happy tear. In the way, Lochlan grasped May's hand and pulled her to the floor for a slow dance. The way Ewan stole Natalie's camera from her, holding it over his head until she gave him a kiss. In the way Dad fist-bumped his twin, Killian, after he and Justin won the second round of darts. In the way Emmy caught his gaze from the dance floor, blowing him a kiss that he pretended to catch.

"So much love," he murmured, repeating Pop Pop's observation, feeling like the most blessed person on the planet.

"It's the Irish in them," Pop Pop said with a twinkle in his eye. "Everyone knows the Irish are passionate, fun-loving, high-spirited, devoted, loving...wild."

Reaching for a pint glass, Padraig walked to the tap and filled it with Guinness before returning to his grandfather, lifting it in a toast. "To the Wild Irish?"

Pop Pop chuckled. "To the Wild Irish."

"Mind a couple of visitors, Pop Pop?"

"For you, my dear. Always. And I know I've said it before, but it bears repeating. I like the sound of the words Pop Pop coming from you." He smiled as Emmy walked in, and she caught him putting the bookmark into one of her novels.

Emmy had called him Mr. Collins right up until the day of her wedding to Padraig, when the dear man put his foot down, insisting he wouldn't walk her down the aisle if she didn't call him Pop Pop. She'd made the switch instantly because she didn't want to take the chance he was serious. She'd called him Pop Pop, he'd offered her his arm, and together the two of them walked down the aisle toward Padraig, who awaited her with so much love in his eyes, it had taken her breath away.

"Haven't you read that one a few times before?" Emmy asked, gesturing toward the book with a tilt of her head.

Pop Pop winked at her. "I've read it at least a dozen times, my sweet girl. It's my favorite of yours. You wrote my story with Sunday so beautifully."

Emmy had asked Pop Pop if he would mind if she penned the story of how he met and fell in love with Sunday. He'd been incredibly touched, and the two of them had spent the better part of two months in this room as he shared memories that Emmy wrote down. The book—his story—was her best-selling book to date, and it was one of the things she was most proud of.

That and...

Emmy glanced down and smiled at her baby daughter, sound asleep in her arms.

Pop Pop holding out his arms expectantly.

Emmy laughed softly as she placed Lila Rose Collins in his arms. She and Padraig had named their daughter after her mother, Lila, and given her Mia's middle name, a namesake for two extraordinary women.

As she often did, Emmy drifted over to Pop Pop's wall of family pictures, looking to see if he'd made any changes since the last time she'd visited. She studied one she hadn't seen of Hunter and Ailis, standing outside their new tour bus, and grinned when she spotted a fun one of Yvonne, getting a piggyback ride on Leo's back at a family picnic last summer.

Then she gasped, spying another picture she'd never seen before. "Where did you get this?"

Pop Pop chuckled but didn't rise, well aware which photograph had caught her eye. "Wondered when you'd see that. I found it by chance."

"Where?"

"On my phone, if you can believe it."

The picture was of her and Padraig the very first time she'd ever been in Pat's Pub. She'd forced herself to walk in that day, fighting through her discomfort of sitting and eating alone in a restaurant. She'd chosen the spot at the end of the bar, hoping it would make her less noticeable, and then she'd set up her laptop even though she'd had no intentions of writing. The laptop had been another layer of distraction, another shield. She thought people who glanced her way would merely assume she was working through her lunch break.

That might have worked with normal people, but neither Padraig nor Pop Pop had ever met a stranger, and she'd been no exception.

"Don't know if you recall or not," Pop Pop went on to explain, "but I'd gotten a brand-new phone that day. Yvonne was waiting tables and when she saw me struggling to figure the darn thing out, she stopped by my stool to show me a few tricks. You and Padraig were chatting, unaware that I was practicing how to use the camera feature with you two as my subjects. That was the very first picture I ever took. I always liked it, so I kept it."

Emmy studied it more closely, looking at it through different eyes. In the photo, Padraig was leaning against the counter directly opposite her, the same way he always did. She was laughing at something he'd said as he smiled.

"Paddy didn't smile a lot back then, but damn if you didn't get a genuine one out of him within minutes. I think that's why I kept the picture originally. Those days, it was rare to see him look so at ease, so happy. Then...I held on to it because it became obvious you were going to be very special to him. To all of us."

Emmy, touched by his kind words, fought hard not to shed happy tears. "You moved down the counter that day and sat next to me, chatting like we were old friends. It was the reason I came back. You made me feel so comfortable, welcome."

"I'm sure I was *one* of the reasons you returned, but you and I both know, the main reason was Paddy."

Emmy acknowledged that truth with a nod. "Guilty as charged."

She started to cross the room to her usual chair, but Pop Pop stopped her. "Hold on a second. I wonder if you might grab that scrapbook from the bottom shelf of the bookcase."

Emmy followed the direction of his gaze, spotting a scrapbook she'd never noticed before. She picked it up and carried it to him. "What is it?"

"Something I've kept tucked away under my bed for the past few years. But I think perhaps it's time you saw it."

Emmy claimed the chair next to him.

"Open it," Pop Pop instructed.

She did as he asked, reading the words written in feminine handwriting on the first page. "The Book of Dreams Come True," she read aloud.

"Mia left it in my care shortly before her death. She asked me to give it to Paddy after she was gone."

"You didn't?" Emmy asked, not bothering to hide her shock. This didn't seem like the sort of thing Pop Pop would keep from his beloved grandson.

"Of course I gave it to him, the day of her memorial service. And over the years, he's come by more than a few times to look at it."

"Why didn't he take it home?"

Pop Pop sighed. "In the beginning, it was too painful for him and I don't think he could cope with the constant reminder of her, or perhaps he just didn't want to look through it alone. It was easier for him to come here, to flip through the pages with me, then tuck it away again. Each time he did, we'd reminisce. At first, the memories were accompanied by tears, but as more time went by, the recollections brought him happiness."

Emmy turned the page. "Oh. Oh wow." Each page contained one of Mia's dreams, the bucket list she and Padraig had worked their way through during their single year together as a couple. Some of the photos she'd seen—the framed ones he'd kept on his wall for years after Mia's death. However, others were new to her.

As she continued to flip through the pages, she realized Mia disappeared from the photos even though it was still her handwriting on top—labeling the dream represented on each page.

"It's still her writing," Emmy observed.

Pop Pop nodded. "Padraig had helped Mia complete her bucket list, but there were still quite a few things on his. She made this scrapbook, leaving the empty pages with the headings so he would move on, would continue to live his life to the fullest. I've taken over adding the pictures."

Emmy saw countless photos of Padraig with different members of his family. He and Colm sitting with their dad at the bar as the Super Bowl played on the big screen behind them. One of he and Finn at a NASCAR race, he and Pop Pop's friend Moose on a fishing trip, holding huge fish aloft and cheesing for the camera, he and Pop Pop standing outside Scully's Pub in Ireland, their arms wrapped around each other's shoulders.

There was one Emmy had taken of him on the Appalachian Trail at the end of a long day of hiking, and one of Padraig, red-faced, his arms held high, as he crossed the finish line of a local marathon he'd run for charity a few months earlier. Emmy had taken that photo at Pop Pop's request without realizing his intentions for it. Some of the pages were still blank, but Emmy made a note of each and every dream listed, determined to find a way to help Padraig fill them with pictures.

Emmy froze when she reached the last two pages of the book—and found photos of herself under the headings "True Love, part two" and "Paddy's Little Girl." On those pages were pictures of Emmy on her own wedding day to Padraig, as well as the day Lila was born.

She wiped away a tear. "Mia was amazing."

"So are you, Emmy. You brought Paddy back to us, and you've made sure that each and every one of his dreams came true."

It took her a moment to find her voice and when she did, all she managed to say was, "Thank you for showing me this."

Pop Pop patted her hand, baby Lila still sound asleep in his other arm. Emmy flipped through the book once more, she and Pop Pop swapping stories about the pictures. Now, like always, whenever Emmy was with Pop Pop, she felt her mother's presence, certain the born storyteller was there with them, loving each and every tale he told just as much as Emmy did.

"Em?" she heard Padraig call from the living room. "You got a second?"

She rose, turning to take Lila from Pop Pop. He shook his head. "Leave her here with me."

Lila was awake now, and Emmy expected she'd begin fussing soon for a clean diaper and a bottle. But for now, she seemed perfectly content in her great-grandfather's arms.

"I'll be right back," Emmy said, but Pop Pop waved her away.

"Take your time."

Emmy had just reached the hall when she heard him whisper to Lila, "Have I ever told you what your name means?"

Did you know? You can SEE HOW IT ALL BEGAN for Padraig and Emmy in Wild Encounter, a Wilder Irish short story, showing the first time Emmy ever walked into Pat's Pub.
You can download it for FREE here.

What's next? Are you ready to read more about those sexy Italian Stallions, the Moretti Brothers from Philadelphia? If so, you're in LUCK!
The first book in this sexy series of menages, Down and Dirty is coming in 2022.
Preorder your copy today!

DEAR READERS

When I first started writing the Wild Irish series in 2009, I had no idea that I would spend the next twelve years of my life immersed in the world of Pat's Pub, nor could I have foreseen just how much I would come to love this family. I swear there are times I have to remind myself they don't really exist!

There are so many moments from my own life reflected in the pages of these books, everything from characters' names to practical jokes to actual dialogue. The "wings etiquette" debate was one I'd seen waged in person between my brother and husband! There are times during rereads where I laugh as I recall the "real life" event that inspired those scenes.

It was my beloved editor, Kelli Collins (see what I did there?), who after reading *Come Monday*, said "I want all the stories." She has walked every step of the Wild Irish journey with me and her wonderful guidance, advice, tough love, and friendship has meant more to me than words could ever express. I commented after finishing the original series that Riley was one of my favorite characters to which she replied,

"That's because you *are* Riley." I'm not sure she realizes how much I considered that an amazing compliment.

Over the years, I've received countless emails and messages from readers about this series. From those who've wished themselves a part of the Collins clan, those who hoped to be struck by that "curse," and those who related to a particular character or story. I was most particularly moved by those of you who wrote to share your own experiences with grief and the loss of a loved one after reading *Wild Devotion*. Your stories, your memories, and your resilience inspired *Wild Chance*. To each of you, you are the sun.

Second chance stories have always been one of my favorite tropes—right up there with friends to lovers—and I desperately wanted Padraig to find love again. I hope I have done you all proud with his and Emmy's story. I knew Padraig was going to need a very special woman after Mia...and then came Emmy, a sweet, compassionate woman who'd suffered her own losses and who understood Paddy (sometimes even better than he understood himself).

When I originally plotted out the next generation's stories, I have to confess I envisioned Pop Pop dying in the last book, his legacy as the wise barman being carried forward by Padraig. However, as the series crept ever closer to December, I knew I couldn't do that. This world needs Pop Pop—his wisdom, his understanding, his compassion, and his unending belief that love (in all its many forms) is the most important thing. And so...he lives forever.

What's next for Mari Carr? Well, obviously...the Moretti family—those sexy Italian Stallions from Philly. And because they have friends and family in Baltimore and because I'm terrible at goodbyes, I think you can count on more than a few Collins cameos in future books.

From the bottom of my heart, I want to thank you...for

your emails, your Facebook messages/posts, and most importantly, your support. I'm raising a pint of Guinness in honor of you!

All the best,
Mari

THE WILDER IRISH SERIES

Have you read the entire Wilder Irish series? All the books are standalone, so they can be read in any order. Be sure to check out all of them!

Wild Passion
Wild Desire
Wild Devotion
Wild at Heart
Wild Temptation
Wild Kisses
Wild Fire
Wild Spirit
Wild Side
Wild Night
Wild Embrace
Wild Dreams
Wild Chance

Fans of Wild Irish AND Facebook! There's a group for you. Come join the Wild Irish Facebook group for sneak peaks, cover reveals, contests and more! Join now.

And be sure to join Mari's newsletter to receive a **FREE** sexy Wilder Irish novella, One Wild Night.

ABOUT THE AUTHOR

Virginia native Mari Carr is a New York Times and USA TODAY bestseller of contemporary romance novels. With over two million copies of her books sold, Mari was the winner of the Romance Writers of America's Passionate Plume award for her novella, Erotic Research. She has over a hundred published works, including her popular Wild Irish and Compass books, along with the Trinity Masters series she writes with Lila Dubois.

Follow Mari:
www.maricarr.com
mari@maricarr.com

Join her newsletter so you don't miss new releases and for exclusive subscriber-only content.

9 781958 056592